THE TREASURE OF GRANZELLA RANCH

A NOVEL

BY

JOAN BANNAN

Author photo by:
AUTUMN AGRELLA PHOTOGRAPHY
http://autumnagrella.wix.com/photos

Map drawn by: Alan James Fikejs

Formatted for Publication by: eBook Launch
https://ebooklaunch.com/

ISBN: 978-0-9627624-5-1 (hc - Large Print)

Library of Congress Control Number: 2017906422

Printed in the United States of America

JB Communications rev. date: 5/21/2017

Dedication

To Anthony Alan "Tony" Mangini

First born son

GENEALOGY

Maurizio Granzella 1901 - 1960
Adelina Russo 1903 - 1958
Married 1920

Roberto (Bob) Granzella 1922 -2013   Mae Granzella 1925 - 1927
Dorothy Burgess 1932 - 2012
Married 1957

Roberto (Rob) Granzella 1960 - 2016
Francesca Bertolli 1962 -
Married 1980

Frances {Franky} Granzella 1968 -
Shirley Baldwin 1972 -
Married 1982 - Divorced 1989
Donna Woodward 1975
Married 1996 - Divorced 1999
Brenna Tootle 1978
Married 2000

Deidre Granzella 1983 -
Thomas March 1981-
Married 2001

Sherre Granzella 1987 -
Charles (Chuck) Shockley 1986-
Married 2010 - Divorced 2016

Courtney March 2002-
Tommy March 2007-

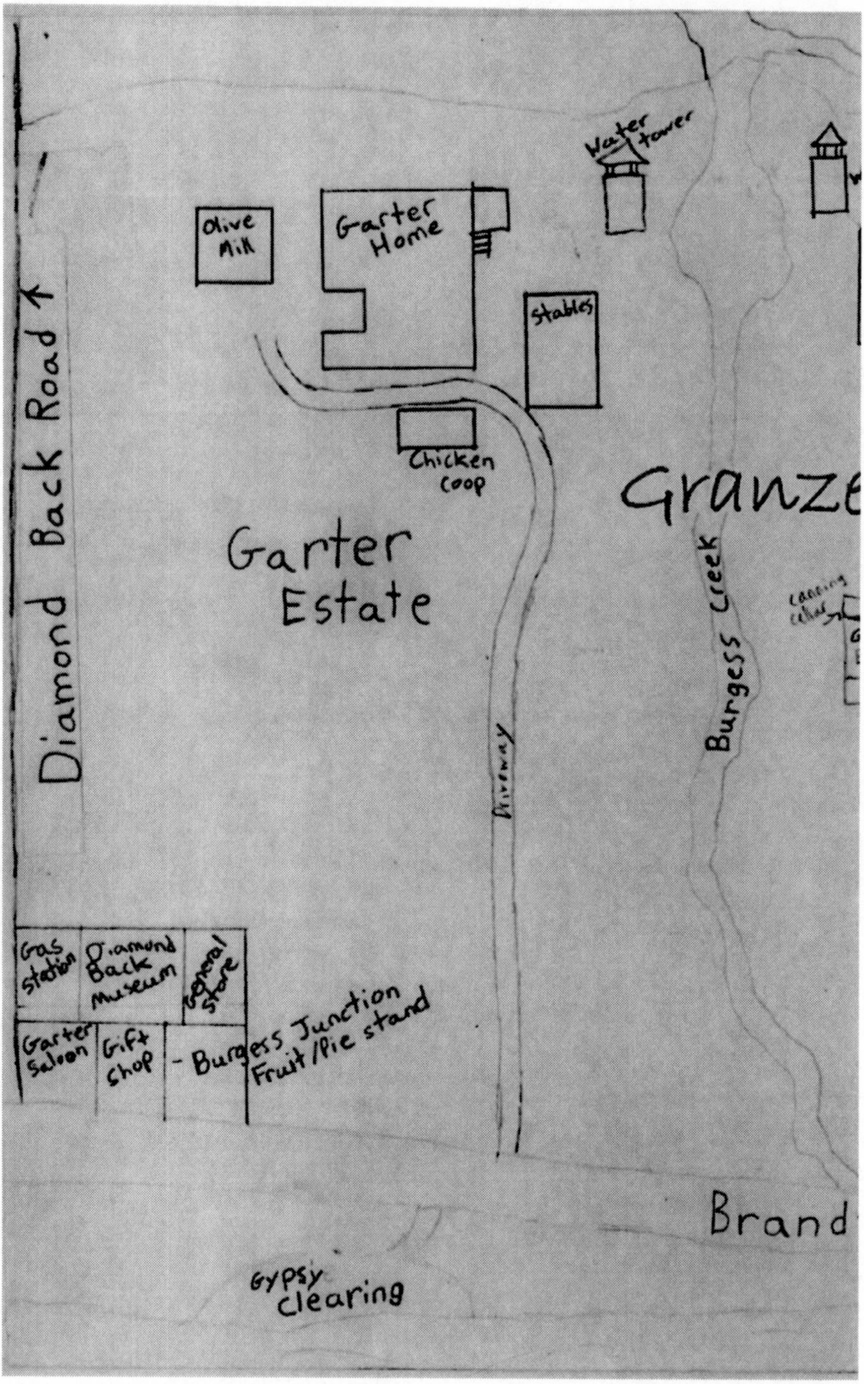
Water tower
Olive Mill
Garter Home
Stables
Chicken coop
Granze
Diamond Back Road
Garter Estate
Burgess Creek
Driveway
Gas station
Diamond Back Museum
General Store
Garter Saloon
Gift Shop
- Burgess Junction Fruit/Pie stand
Brand
Gypsy Clearing

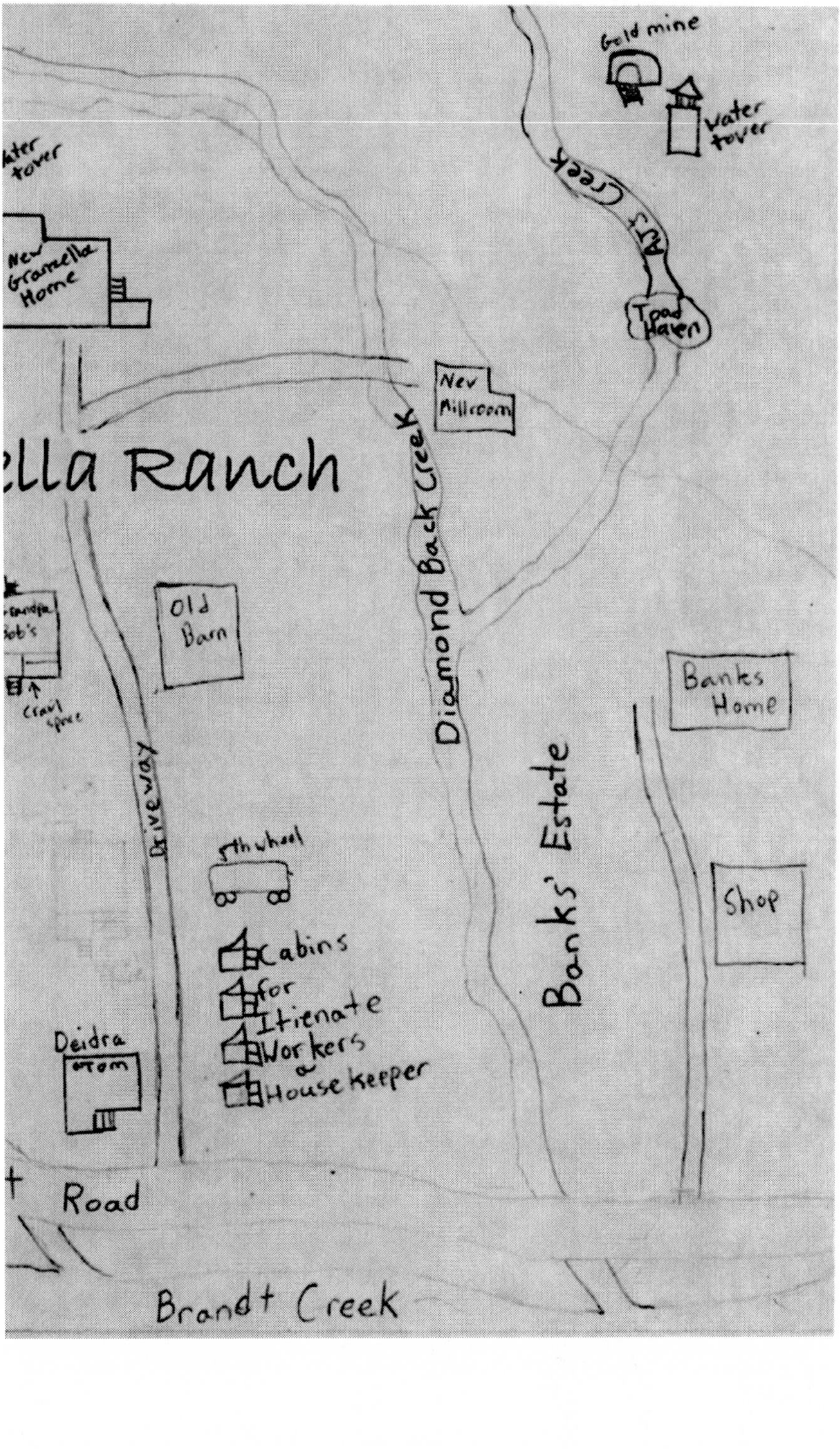

Gold mine
Vater tover
Ant Creek
Toad Haven
ater tower
New Granzella Home
New Millroom
ella Ranch
Diamond Back Creek
Old Barn
Banks Home
Banks' Estate
Driveway
5th wheel
Shop
Cabins for Itienate Workers & House keeper
Deidra & Tom
Road
Brandt Creek

CHAPTER ONE

Trouble at the Ranch

As she stepped out of her car, Sherre Granzella Shockley was blasted with a body slam followed by a hug.

"Aunt Sherre!"

Tommy's sister, Courtney, stood patiently behind him for a few seconds before tapping him on the shoulder, "My turn."

Turning Tommy slightly, Sherre said, "Oh Courtney, there's room for both of you." She extended her other arm to enclose the rigid body of her niece. "Group hug." Enjoying the near-tearful emotion, she hugged them closer and said, "Boy, I've missed you two." Then letting them go to hold one of each of their hands, "How can you have grown so much in only nine months?"

"It's the olive oil," Courtney stated flatly. "That's what Grandma says."

"Of course it is." Sherre and Tommy giggled. Courtney smiled her awkward grin.

Sherre said, "It's so kind of both of you to show up just in time to help me unload this overstuffed car." She lifted her right eyebrow and smiled as if to say, "Please?"

"Um, well yeah, we could do that, right Courtney?" replied Tommy, "And, here comes Mom!"

Sherre reached her sister at the point where the path between the Picholine and Manzanilla olive orchards intersected the gravel driveway. Deidre stopped chugging up the hill to step into her sister's open arms. Sherre felt Deidre's fluttery, irregular breathing.

Deidre whispered into Sherre's ear, "He's here."

She looked toward her mother's house on the plateau above. "I thought that Cadillac might be his. Did he know I was coming?"

"Probably. I'm sure he wants to start charming you as soon as possible." Deidre took a shuddering breath. "Okay. Let's unload your boxes into Grandpa's house first, and then I'll introduce you to the fiancé, Darian Danville." She employed a mocking tone when pronouncing his name. "He's trying to manipulate Mom into picking a date really, really soon."

Sherre countered, "Yikes, this is happening so fast! Is there a ring?"

"No, not yet, but they are both referring to him as her fiancé."

"Is he living here?"

Deidre snorted, "No."

"You scoff, and yet, if she's referring to him as her fiancé—gosh, Mom has barely mentioned that she's seeing someone. Maybe she'll open up to me now that I'm back." Sherre kept one arm around her sister. "Are you sure you're ready to keep climbing this driveway, Deedee?"

"I'm so out of shape. I need to start working out or at least start walking regularly. I was hoping to be slimmer by the time you saw me again."

"Why? You're always gorgeous to me."

"Thank you. I know, I know." Sherre recognized a hot blend of hope and pain that darted quickly through her sister's eyes. "You

3

always say things like that and you mean them, but—" Sherre sensed she was holding something back, however, Deidre stayed on topic, "I can't seem to get rid of the 'baby weight'" She laughed nervously. "Seems like fourteen years since the first one and nine years since the second would be enough time. It was just a goal, you know—two more months until Sherre comes home, so in two months I should be able to lose three or four pounds. You, on the other hand, look dreadfully thin."

"It's called the Divorce Diet." She grinned defensively, but her voice wavered. "It's universally effective. All you have to do is to come home from a business trip and find a sexy woman wearing your robe, serving breakfast to your husband in your kitchen." She waved her hand as if it contained a magic wand. She hoped it would wave away the threat of tears. "Instantly, you have no appetite." The pain of missing Charles welled up like a knot somewhere near her heart. A knot deftly entwined with threads of humiliation and rejection. Sherre was still very much in denial. She replayed a mental sound bite, *this is not happen-*

ing to me. She hadn't lost her determination. In the depths of her soul there was an inkling of confidence that she could still restore her marriage.

"Oh no! You didn't tell me that part."

Sherre said, "Yeah. I guess my sense of shame is proportionate, not just to the embarrassment of his rejection, but also to the number of people who know about it."

"It's not *your* shame, Sherre! I'm so sorry. I didn't realize I was bringing it up. I told myself I wouldn't unless you wanted to talk about it." Then angrily, Deidre said, "That creep. He's got to be stupidest man on earth."

"Yeah," Sherre chuckled nervously, "that's the way I feel, but unfortunately, he's probably not."

"He might be. I wonder if he has even *seen* you!" Deidre's voice accelerated to a higher emotional pitch, "You are one of the most beautiful women on the planet and on top of that you're so smart and accomplished. You can fix anything!"

Sherre grinned, "I keep telling myself that."

"All those companies you've reorganized and restored to prosperity... How'd it go? Did you get that dairy supply company back into the black?"

"Yeah. I did." Sherre smiled and nodded a few times. "I got so caught up whining to you about my homecoming, I forgot to tell you that Fort Worth went remarkably well. After they paid my hefty consulting fee, they sent me away with the promise of a nice bonus in the first quarter of next year if—when," she smiled again, "they reap their projected profits. I'll bore you with all the details later if you want, but," grabbing a box marked "BEDROOM" from the trunk of her car, caringly, she asked, "do you feel up to helping with these boxes?"

"Sure. I lift things all the time: Groceries, beds, vacuums, buckets. It's stamina I'm lacking." Deidre picked up one labeled, "KITCHEN," and followed her sister up the two tilting steps leading to the open door to their late grandfather's rustic farmhouse.

"Hey, Deedee," Sherre set down the box onto the floor next to the freshly made bed.

"Thank you! You must have been cleaning up this old place for weeks."

Deidre came into the bedroom with Tommy close on her heels. "Great to have you back. No one's called me Deedee around here since you left."

"Can I call you Deedee?"

"No sweetheart. There are only two people in the world with the privilege to call me Mom. Please stick with the program, Tommy."

"Okay." Not allowing the ban to squash his enthusiasm. "We *all* cleaned and cleaned, Aunt Sherre."

"Yeah. The kids worked really hard," Deidre patted Tommy on the shoulder, "and Mom came down a few times. We mucked out the cupboards, dusted until we couldn't sneeze anymore, and killed at least a million spiders. We lined the cupboards and closet shelves with bug-inhibiting shelf-paper, unpacked the boxes you shipped ahead, and put stuff away as well as we thought you'd like. I did this room." She grinned. "You like?"

"I do like!" She stepped over to the tiny golden nugget that her sister chose to place in a glass bowl on top of the mahogany dresser. She picked it up and smiled. It was shaped like a lumpy pyramid.

"What's that?" Tommy burst past his mom. "Can I hold it?"

Sherre set the heavy-for-its-size nugget into his open palm. "It's probably just fool's gold. When we were kids, my friend, Johnny, found it near the mine on the other side of Diamond-back Ridge."

Tommy stared at the nugget and started giggling uncontrollably.

Sherre's first laugh emerged as a honk. Having no idea what was so hysterically amusing didn't hinder her. She had always found Tommy's laughter contagious, especially when he was a toddler. Her giggles fueled his to a new level and set Deidre laughing as well. He wrapped his fingers around the nugget and fell back on the bed.

"What's so funny? Courtney had come into the room. She looked entertained by her mother, aunt, and brother, all completely out of control.

Deidre breathlessly said, "It's something Tom said last night—"

Tommy stuck his arm into the air, holding the nugget high, and took a gasping breath. He broke from laughing long enough to say, "And! It looks like a pile of horse dung!" Then he snickered, pulling the nugget to his belly as he hugged himself into more laughter.

Courtney commented sensibly, "Dad told Mom last night, 'No matter how talented your sister is at fixing things, the only way she'll be able save Granzella Ranch will be if she can poop a bucket of gold nuggets.'"

CHAPTER TWO

The Fiancé

Sherre and Deidre knocked on the door of the house in which they'd grown up. Courtney and Tommy stood patiently behind, all of them feeling awkward. Before their grandmother had a boyfriend hanging out here, they would just tap a few times and walk right in.

Darian welcomed them in as if it were his home, not theirs. "Come in, come in."

He gave Sherre a wolfish smile and held the screen door, in a manner that forced them to brush his body as they entered. Sherre empathized particularly with Courtney who had always been uncomfortable with physical contact.

Sherre's stomach churned as Darian raked her with his gaze. She scrutinized him too, but with more discretion. He was dressed richly to accent his tall, slight build. His dark brown hair was styled longer on top. One careless, or perhaps contrived, lock fell in a wave on one side of his high forehead. His nails were blocked and clean. He had a strong jaw, contemptuous mouth and gray, distant eyes, surrounded by thin, short lashes. His eyebrows, though, were thick and pronounced. He moved with suave arrogance.

Francesca's entrance from the kitchen disrupted the awkwardness. She had hugs for all, starting with her younger daughter, who was sometimes mistaken for her twin. It wasn't that Sherre looked old. It was that Francesca had barely aged. She spent time to stay fit. She spent money on vitamins and excellent skin care. She never left her bedroom without dressing appropriately for her day: her hair, makeup, and earrings perfection. The resemblance between them was so striking, Sherre blushed when people remarked about her mother's beauty.

"So, Sherre, you've met Darian?"

"Um sort of. Hello, Darian." In spite of a disturbing energy she felt from Darian, Sherre was pleased to see her mother more radiant than she could remember. She was certainly happier than the last time they were together at her father's funeral nine months ago. The sadness on Francesca's face had lifted. Sherre was pleased that her mom could find happiness, but leery of this man who was closer in age to her own age than to her mother's. He was, reportedly, only four years older than Deidre. She knew, of course, that these negative feelings were predictable. It was challenging to accept *anyone* replacing her father in her mother's affections, but she felt more mistrustful than resentful.

"So you are the accomplished Sherre, the fixer maven." He gave her a skeptical, yet flirty stare, "Coming home to save the family ranch."

"I hope so. That's the plan anyway."

Francesca interrupted, "Come in, come into the family room. I made some fresh lemonade and iced tea."

"I want both," said Tommy. "Dad calls it an Arnold Palmer."

Francesca smiled. "Yes, Tommy. Your dad's favorite drink was my inspiration." She gave him a sideways hug.

Sherre settled at the large, farmhouse dining table instead of stepping down to the sunken family room. Everyone followed her lead, pulled out chairs, and gathered around. She strategically chose a seat facing the wall of paned glass windows and French doors that looked across the property. Level with her mom's house on the ridge was the relatively new building that housed their gleaming, state-of-the-art, Pieralisi olive mill. Sherre shuddered as the balloon payment came to mind. *I still have time though. It's months away. I can fix this.* Beneath the ridge, the cloudy heads of the great olives sailed between the rich, sandy soil and the brazen bowl of summer sky above. The hot, July breeze rocked the green-silver trees until they resembled a flowing river. Nostalgia stirred within her, marred by a thin thread of fear. Four generations of acquiring land and building an olive oil business were in jeopardy. Several of their orchards were planted in the late 1800s before her great-grandfather moved here. After the California Gold Rush subsided, migrants settled here to mine other-than-gold riches in this magnificent Calaveras Hill Country. She said out loud, "So, there's an offer from Denny Garter?"

"Yes," said Francesca. "He says if we sell, he'll sub-divide and let us carve out our homes—not yours, Sherre, Grampa Bob's house is entwined with the orchards, but he said he would grant deed Tom and Deidre's down by the road and grant a right of way to my driveway so I could stay here."

"What about the well?"

"We'd need a right of way to that too. Denny emphasized that he'd hire us to continue caring for the trees, harvesting, and run the mill for him. And he said we could still mill for the small ranchers too." She sighed. "In the middle of the night, my mind is like a hamster in search of a wheel. We could move the fifth wheel up here close to the house, but the cabins your grandpa built for the itinerate workers are all on the property Denny wants. And of course, my mind keeps circling back to the balloon payment. If we could just pay that and get through this next harvest—"

Sherre groaned a, "Hmmm," and then poured herself an Arnold Palmer from the two pitchers. "What'd you tell him?"

Her mom reached her hand across the table to put it on top of Sherre's, "I told him you were coming home and we'd talk about it. I told him he'd need to be patient for an answer." She nodded toward Deidre. "Tom says it's going to be a good harvest this year, unlike the paltry crop we harvested last year." She grumbled, "This drought!—If we can time the harvest and mill it before a deep freeze, we might be able to make a comeback."

"Maybe. But we'll need some capital to get that far. You're right about that darned payment. He couldn't help dying could he?" Sherre noticed that Darian squirmed in his chair. "I need to ferret out our options. It's not enough to cover it, but I'm willing to infuse the money from my last two corporate rescue operations. That's if Chuck doesn't come after it." She felt her neck get red. "And, if I can come up with a large enough chunk of it, I may be able to secure a small business loan."

"Oh Honey! No. You shouldn't sink your own money into the business that may still fail. Maybe Denny will give us a loan instead of taking us over," Francesca offered.

"I don't trust him." This from Deidre.

"I don't know. It sounds like he's trying to be fair. But, if we trust him to buy us out of this financial mess, I'm not sure we can trust him to keep our reputation. The rest of the world is beginning to recognize the excellence of California olive oils, just as it did with California wine. The Olive Oil Council, the rest of industry, and the community, expects integrity from Granzella Ranch. If he'd loan to us without strings, maybe." She grimaced. "There's got to be another way. The way he's run his own olive oil business—" She turned to Darian, "A few years ago he imported bulk oil from Australia and sold it as local estate olive oil. It's something that's easy to do because he has so many trees. People assumed he was being truthful, but when it was tested and tasted, it tainted the reputation of the spectacular oil from trees in the entire area. It makes me wonder how he runs the rest of his little Calaveras Empire."

Darian's face sparked interest, "Empire?"

Deidre answered, "Yeah. He owns pretty much everything in Brandt, including that strip mall down at the intersection of Brandt and Diamondback Roads. He leases to the owners of the market, the gas station, and the small shops, but he personally runs the Garter Saloon."

"And now he wants to own us too," said Sherre.

"Especially you," said Deidre.

"Really?" Darian looked amused.

Francesca replied, "He's always been sweet on Sherre. He didn't have a chance with her in high school, not that he didn't try. This may be an attempt to avenge his pride because she blew him off and married Chuck Shockley."

"Ah, I see. A woman in great demand." Darian smirked and once again inspected Sherre in a manner she considered inappropriate. "And valuable property at risk."

Sherre felt her cheeks turn fiery and checked for a similar reaction from her mother. "Or maybe he just wants to own everything of value in this community."

Darian lifted one eyebrow. "Maybe he'll make a generous offer and you'll all retire with a fortune."

Tommy finished his Arnold Palmer with a noisy slurp which caused his mother to shoot him a disapproving look. "Can I go home now?"

"Sure, if your sister wants to go with you."

Courtney nodded. "Yes. I do." She glanced up at the clock on the wall. "It's time for me to practice piano. Ninety minutes today."

"Courtney, will you take the meat out of the refrigerator and set it on the counter, please? It's sitting on a plate. You'll see it. I'll be down in a little bit."

They heard a yelp when the children got to the door. Courtney shot back to the kitchen filled with enthusiasm, eyes wide, "Ah, er—" she waved her hand nervously toward the door. "Johnny Depp is coming up the driveway. He has a dog with him."

CHAPTER THREE

Johnny

Johnny, the youngest of twelve children, would not have been born had his mother, Aislyn, succeeded in her superstitious attempts to abort him. Early in her pregnancy, she secretly drank tea brewed with Pennroyal, Black Cohosh, and Mugwort. When her husband was away from camp, she'd wander through graveyards, hoping to cross over graves containing victims of suicide. In spite of these and other naïve efforts, in the summer of 1986, Aislyn was great with child and nearing her delivery date. Aislyn's family, and the five other Irish Gypsy families with whom they were traveling, circled their RVs, fifth wheels, and vans in a clearing near a creek in Brandt, California.

Two weeks before the baby arrived, Aislyn maneuvered her heavy belly and six of her children down the dirt road from their camp and across a meadow to buy produce at the Burgess Fruit Stand. Another Burgess customer, Lois Banks, introduced herself as the carpenter's wife. Aislyn smiled broadly and thanked Lois for the kindness her husband had shown them. Their first week in Brandt, Aislyn's husband sought work from John Banks at his cabinet shop. John hired him to sharpen tools and bought several restored gadgets from him, including a soldered, antique tea kettle. John said he'd always wanted something like that out in the shop.

Lois made dove noises as she asked each of the children to tell her their names. They all spoke at once interrupting each other, vying for the nice lady's attention. They volunteered that there were five siblings back at the camp. "Eleven children!" She sheepishly asked Aislyn if it would offend anyone if she bought each of them a treat.

While picking out packets of beef jerky, dried fruits, and shelled nuts, Lois gushed over Aislyn also. Lois looked at Aislyn's enormous middle, smiled bravely and wiped away a tear before confessing that she and her husband had always wanted children, but it was no longer a possibility.

After Aislyn and the children left, Lois noticed Emily giggling behind the cash register. "Lois, don't worry. There's no way you're insulting a gypsy by giving gifts."

Lois nodded. "Well then, dried fruit and nuts are not enough!" She generously filled several shopping bags with potatoes, sweet potatoes, carrots, melons, and a variety of summer squash. She added a bearful of local honey, four loaves of ciabatta bread, and two of the famous homemade fruit pies that attracted buyers from all points of Calaveras County and beyond. She spotted the waddling mother and her train of ducklings where the dirt road plunged beneath the shade of huge oak trees. Aislyn set down her plastic bag full of produce and began to massage her lower back. She protested politely as she surveyed the bounty in the trunk of Lois' car.

Lois insisted that she take the food, saying, "The Lord has always provided generously for me and now He has provided for you." She handed bags to each of the children then pulled a bottle of olive oil from a crisscrossed, cardboard box in her trunk. "Here. The Granzellas milled these for us." She waved her arm toward the olive oil ranch and her own home across Brandt Road up on the ridge beyond the gypsy camp. She grinned proudly. "This oil is from our own trees. God bless you and your lovely family."

Aislyn bowed her head and mumbled as she crossed herself.

When Aislyn went into labor, her husband was conveniently away, scouting for work. The conspiring midwife left the newborn baby on Lois' front porch. Through the open window, Lois thought it odd to hear a feral cat wailing during daylight hours so she found the still sticky infant immediately. He was tightly swaddled in a ragged towel and surrounded by a makeshift bassinet fashioned from a torn bed sheet and a cardboard box. A note, scribbled on a piece of paper grocery sack read, "To the carpenter and his wife. I want you to adopt my baby. Please raise this boy for me. The Lord has provided." Lois Banks knew, of course, who "me" was. She called her husband, John, in from his shop and sent him straight away to the market for baby formula, bottles, and disposable diapers. As soon as he left, she gently washed the baby in warm water and gentle, homemade, olive oil soap. All the while the boy howled. She swaddled him in a soft towel and marched him around her living room trying to explain to him, and convince herself, that everything would be okay. She prayed it would be. When John returned, he called the Sheriff.

By the time the Sheriff arrived, the gypsy camp was empty. Because the note clearly indicated the parent's intention, and because he personally endorsed the Banks, he talked a friend at Child Services into "deputizing" the Banks as foster parents until they could be formally vetted. The small community helped John and Lois expedite the procedure to acquire a foster care license. Soon after, the Banks pursued the foster-to-adopt process.

They named him John after his father, but he was ever, Johnny. From the first moment of extinguishing Johnny's screaming with a bottle of formula, Lois doted over her precious son with large portions of delicious meals. Her love language was food. Throughout Johnny's childhood and adolescence, he was pudgy. He wasn't exactly bullied, but he was often separate from most of the children, occasionally mocked, but primarily, ignored. One person befriended him and he loved her.

The property line between the Banks' land and Granzella Ranch was Diamondback Creek. Most often it was Sherre who crossed over to the Banks' estate. She and Johnny explored the hills above, hour upon hour. Lois fully stocked their backpacks with sandwiches, cookies, and water so they could continue their adventures, often until there was barely enough sunlight to see their way home on the path adjacent to the creek.

After a wet winter, the creek ran freely throughout the summer, waning to a trickle in the fall. Sherre and Johnny had a favorite spot where the creek flowed through a wooded area. A fallen tree trunk served as a creekside bench with a view of a tiny waterfall, created by a branch from the toppled tree that bridged the water. Midsummer of one dry year, cut off from the flowing creek water, a small pond formed at the foot of their bench.

"Look Johnny. Polliwogs! Aw. They're so wiggly and cute."

"Must be hundreds of them."

"The water is way less than yesterday. This is going to dry up before they get their legs. Let's dig a trench to route some of the water from the creek."

Johnny grinned. "Let's not."

"You're so mean. You think it's funny that they'll all die?"

"No. They won't die. They'll grow their legs faster as the water gets lower. Trust me. We'll check on them every day and when the water's almost gone, if they don't have their legs, we can still rescue them, but you'll see." He grinned again. "And, we have a control group. By the way, I think these are tadpoles, not polliwogs."

"What's the difference?"

"Frogs and toads."

"Oh. What's a control group, and why are you such an expert on amphibians?"

"My dad lets me use his computer."

"Lucky."

"There's lots of stuff to look up. I found one website called The Knowledge Network Explorer. It has all kinds of stories about all kinds of things, mostly for middle school kids like us. So anyway, a control group is another set of subjects in the same situation as the test group, but with one difference. Those little guys, stuck above the branch in the pooled water, still have the creek flowing over them. They can be the control group. They have all the water they need to stay fish. I'd bet most of those won't even get their back legs by the time our little guys that are running out of water have all four legs and start climbing out."

"Cool."

Each day throughout the next week, Johnny and Sherre checked the shrinking pond to observe the tadpoles' progress. First they grew their strong, angled back legs. As the water got scarcer, the front legs popped out. There were fewer and fewer tadpoles in the small pool each time they came. The toads climbed out without waiting for their tails to recede. As Johnny predicted, before the water was gone from the diminishing pond, all of the tadpoles that lived there morphed into toads and only a few of the tadpoles in the larger body of water had begun to grow back legs. The day they visited the empty, muddy pond, there were little toads everywhere, slurping up miniscule bugs that swarmed in the deep grass at the base of the log.

"Oh Johnny. Look how cute." Sherre scooped up three tiny toads and separated her fingers so Johnny could look into her palms.

"Yeah, amazingly cute." She failed to notice that he wasn't looking at the toads.

"It's kind of like they're our children." She set the little toads back onto the thick grass. "But, it's a good thing they're not."

"Why's that?"

"We'd never be able to think up enough names for all of them."

Johnny's laugh sounded like a soft machinegun. Sherre laughed too.

He was plagued with mild acne and felt awkward and unworthy, so Johnny listened as a best friend when Sherre dealt with an onslaught of attention from the opposite sex during high school. From catalogs, he helped her choose which dress she would wear to the Junior Prom for her date with Denny Garter, and then again a year later, when she went to the Senior Ball with Chuck Shockley. Too afraid and shy to proclaim his love for her, Johnny waved goodbye to Sherre as she left with Chuck to attend a private college in Los Angeles. Four years later, Sherre and Chuck took marriage vows beneath the midsummer olive boughs.

When Sherre left town the first time, John gave his son a bloodhound puppy hoping the slobbery, boundy dog would ease the pain in Johnny's aching heart. Johnny named his new companion, Captain Jack Sparrow, and began training him as a search dog. When Sherre left town the second time as Chuck's wife, he took Captain Jack up to the waterfall. He sat down on their log. Jack laid his head on his paws and listened sympathetically as Johnny told him how much he missed Sherre and how this no longer seemed like home. Jack seemed to agree with Johnny that it was time for them to leave.

They began their mission as "Rescue for Hire" in Colorado. They spent the next four years traveling the United States looking for kidnap victims, lost hunters, and escaped convicts. With Jack's big broad snout and a sense of smell many thousand times greater than humans, he could track a person for miles and pick him out of a crowded room. Johnny trained him to recognize the smell of human remains and find them even under water. He and Jack attended bloodhound training seminars and sometimes returned home to Brandt to run drills on the Banks' estate and the surrounding wooded foothills of Calaveras County. The bond between man and dog was fervent. Johnny felt Jack's sense of pride and accomplishment when he'd sniff at clothing and track ribbons of scent through acres of rough terrain, and then stand at attention near the uncovered quarry. Jack learned not to bark lest he give away his position while tracking criminal suspects. After they returned to the

States from a seminar at the International Bloodhound Training Institute in Italy, Johnny's mobile phone rarely stopped ringing. On the road, Captain Jack rode in the passenger seat of Johnny's pickup. When they stopped to rest, Jack watched TV with Johnny in the evenings. He would smile and chatter his teeth to let Johnny know he wanted a cookie. Johnny always stayed at pet-friendly motels so they could both rest comfortably. Johnny thought of Captain Jack Sparrow as his silent partner, an extension of himself, only Johnny considered Jack the wiser partner.

Rescue for Hire was enormously popular. Not only did a search dog make a huge difference in an investigation, but Johnny normally asked only for expenses and often charged nothing. John Banks made Johnny a joint trustee in the substantial living trust that he had inherited from his father and grandfather. The skillful carpenter and cabinet maker of Calaveras County earned an abundant living, but never actually needed to. He encouraged his son to pursue his passion without regard to compensation.

On his treks with Captain Jack Sparrow, Johnny's black Irish features weathered handsomely. His skin turned unblemished and perpetually tan. Away from his mother's delicious menus and baked goods, he slimmed his six foot frame to a taut, lean one-seventy-five. He found contentment as he and Jack helped people find lost loved ones, in spite of the fact that they rarely assisted in an actual rescue. More often, they were commissioned with giving families closure by confirming tragedy.

Then, in the spring of their fourth search-and-rescue year, Johnny faced two tragedies of his own.

A private investigator, Bob Adams, with whom Johnny and Jack had worked in Minnesota called one morning to ask if they could come to a rural area north of Brainerd to assist in the search for a nineteen year old woman, Amy Cunningham. Johnny reluctantly agreed. Jack seemed to be exhausted from their three month hunt through snowbanks along frozen rivers for a twenty-one year old brunette. Humans found her body, but they insisted that

Captain Jack had led them into the right neighborhood.

When Johnny and Jack arrived at Amy's search site, law-enforcement officials welcomed all volunteers, but some were troubled by the attention news reporters allotted to Rescue for Hire and other freelance searchers. Several bloodhound owners showed up, along with psychics and dowsers with divining rods. They began a tedious search that covered hundreds of square miles. Johnny and Jack kept searching after the other freelancers gave up. They eventually narrowed their search to an expanse of land between Blue Trout River and the highway. They gained permission from property owner, Arthur Brown, to search on his land where Captain Jack Sparrow wanted to take them.

In a large wooded area, Johnny freed Captain Jack to work off the leash. Jack lowered his nose to the ground to zigzag as if following a scent. He emerged from the timber into a meadow. A strong northern wind blasted across the meadow and Jack took off into it. Johnny fired up his truck. The sheriff deputies and the remaining volunteers, jumped into two four-wheel drive vehicles. They raced to where they'd lost sight of Jack. When it became impossible to continue on, the majority of searchers returned for horses. Johnny continued on foot under the gloom of tangled woods. A thick bed of twigs crunched beneath his boots as he trod through spikes of undergrowth. A dagger-like branch sliced his arm as he squeezed between the trunks of two massive trees. Through a narrow, uneven pathway, he grabbed a jagged branch to keep his balance and scraped his palm raw. The ground beneath his boots began to wobble, so he sat on a log to wait for the mounted horsemen. He spotted them coming from the opposite direction across the bog. They'd realized from Arthur's map that Jack's search area was closer to the highway.

Deputy Sheriff Henry Baldwin, donned chest waders, slipped a second set of waders into a plastic bag, and slogged across the swamp to Johnny. Breathing heavily from his trek through the murky water, he sat next to Johnny on the log and sighed, "We found

Amy. Actually, Captain Jack Sparrow found her. He was lying next to her remains."

"Lying? Not standing pointing?"

"Right. In fact, he seemed to be totally whipped. Jared and I carried him back to your truck. We left your engine running and turned the heater on. He didn't seem up to calling shotgun," Henry grinned, "So we heaved him into the back seat of your double cab. We brought your truck 'round to the highway from there," he nodded toward the thicket though which Johnny had struggled.

"Thanks and thanks."

Jack was lethargically waiting for Johnny. He tapped his tail a few times to acknowledge him, then slept all the way back to the motel where they both ate, slept, and then stayed several days to rest. Warm and resting, Jack seemed to perk up a bit, but he continued to sleep more than normal.

Hundreds of people crowded into Lakeside Evangelical Free Church. Amy's family wanted to pay tribute not only to twenty-one year old Amy, but also to the dozens of law enforcement officers and hundreds of neighbors and friends who had searched for her over the course of eight months. In the front pew, seated on the floor next to Johnny, was Captain Jack Sparrow.

When the funeral was over, unsure if his dog was exhausted or forlorn, he took him to a vet, who determined Jack had a bacterial infection. He was on the vet's aluminum table with his head resting on his paws, too tired to make the effort to live. Johnny reached down to stroke his soft, silky ears. Jack lifted his head to accept his caress, then he laid it down again on his paws to rest forever.

He called Arthur Brown and requested permission to bury his heroic bloodhound in the meadow where Jack caught Amy's scent. Early the next morning, Johnny arrived at the meadow surprised and grateful to see Arthur had arrived before him with his backhoe. After reversing his truck close to the deep hole in the earth, he looked out the front windshield to see two sheriff SUVs approaching. Henry, Jared, and the other three deputies who accompanied Jack on his last search, helped Johnny lower Captain Jack Sparrow's shrouded remains into the ground. They stood with Johnny as Arthur used the tractor to cover the grave.

Filled with grief, Johnny questioned, *what now? Where will I go?* He climbed up into his truck and sat for a moment to think. He reached across the seat for his cell phone and saw that he'd missed several calls from his mother. His father had suffered a fatal heart attack during the night. He left immediately to be with his mother.

He bought another bloodhound puppy and began search dog training with the Banks' Estate as homebase.

"Come on in, Johnny." His appearance had changed so drastically, Sherre thoroughly understood Courtney's confusion. She opened the screen door. "You too," she said to Johnny's new bloodhound, respectfully seated back on its haunches. At her invitation, the dog enthusiastically entered the room. She turned to Johnny, "This can't be Captain Jack?"

Johnny shook his head softly. "No, Jack died about two years ago. Same time as Dad.

He reached down to rub one of the long, silky ears. "This guy is Marcus Aurelius."

"Oh, I'm so sorry. I was in Texas—"

"I know. I'm sorry about your dad too. When I heard about your dad, Marcus and I were training in Georgia—"

"I know."

They stared at each other for a moment, awakening years of camaraderie, familiarity, and intimacy. They nodded in unison. They did know.

"Johnny, you may not remember my niece, Courtney, or maybe I should say *recognize* my niece, Courtney, since she's so grown up now at fourteen. She thought you were someone else."

Johnny grinned mischievously. "Yeah. Depp, right? I get that a lot."

Courtney standing wide-eyed as if at military attention, stated matter-of-factly, "Marcus Aurelius. A Roman emperor and a philosopher." Then, she too reached down to caress Marcus' soft fur.

Johnny was impressed and said so. "You know your history. You must be a good student."

"That is correct." Courtney stood rigidly with her arms at her side. "I'll go now."

Sherre hugged Courtney. "I'll see you tomorrow, yeah? And you too, Tommy."

Tommy had gone to the kitchen and returned with a cookie held in each hand. He extended one to his sister. "Mom said we could have one. It'll be a while 'til dinner."

"Tommy, this is my friend Johnny. I'm not sure if you remember him."

"Johnny of the golden nugget?"

"Yes."

Tommy, freed from one cookie, extended his hand to Johnny, who shook it. "Do you know where more gold nuggets are?"

Marcus fixated on the lowest cookie. Drool began to slide out of one side of his mouth.

Johnny said, "That's the big question, right? Doesn't everyone want to believe there's still gold in our hills?"

Sherre sighed. "We sure could use a cartload of motherlode gold."

Johnny nodded. "Yeah. I heard that too."

"Okay, Tommy." Courtney said mechanically to her brother. "Let's go now."

"Okay." Tommy noticed Marcus and the drool. "Hi boy! I think you want my cookie!"

Johnny said, "Don't fall for it. He's well-fed. He'd con us out of all of our people food if he could get away with it."

"Goodbye. I need to go practice the piano. Come on, Tommy"

Johnny, Tommy, and Sherre all said, "Bye," simultaneously.

Sherre called back toward the kitchen, "Mom, Johnny Banks is here. We're going out to sit on the porch for a while.

"Johnny, may I ask you a favor?"

"I wish you would."

"Could you center this heavy table? I think it got moved over here for the reception after my dad's memorial and it never got put back. Thanks. This is where my chair belongs." Marcus waited until Sherre sat in her favorite wicker chair before he settled his huge head onto her feet.

Johnny moved the other chair to its proper place on the other side of the table said, "He likes you."

"Apparently." She smiled. "I like him too. So Johnny, how'd you know I was home?"

"Your grandmother's remarkable car. I can't believe you're still driving it."

"Yup. Over three-hundred thousand miles and counting. She'd have more if I'd been home more often in the past five years."

"Besides. I heard you were coming."

"And you came right away."

"And I came right away." He grinned.

"So you like me too."

"Yeah." He chuckled. "Marcus and I both like you. How've you been?"

"Oh, you know. Besides being frightened that we'll lose the olive oil business and the land that's been in our family for four generations, I'm broken-hearted, angry, and feeling rejected because my marriage failed."

"Not everyone is going to reject you."

"I dunno. I think that if I couldn't make it with Chuck, I'm probably incapable of making it with anyone. And, you know me better than anyone. I always said that if I got married, it would only be once."

"Yes. I remember."

"So, how are you? How's your mom?"

"I'm good. Mom's good. She said to tell you, 'hi,' and that as soon as you're settled, she'd love to cook up your favorite beef stew and buttermilk cornbread. Everyone knows what's going on, you know."

"Of course they do." she said comfortably, "what else is there to do around here?"

"Well, Mom also said to tell you, 'The Lord will provide.'"

CHAPTER FOUR

Family Restoration

The receding crackle of tires on gravel was the sound for which Sherre had waited. Finally, her mother was alone.

"Sherre! Come in, come in. What're you doing up so late, honey? I'd have thought you'd be exhausted, your long drive, your first day back, unpacking—"

"I am, Mom, but I wanted to talk to you without, er, everyone around."

"You mean Darian, right?"

"Yes, Darian, but Deedee too. What's going on with her that she's not telling me? Is everything okay between her and Tom?"

A muscle twitched at the corner of Francesca's mouth. "No. I mean, I don't know about Deidre and Tom, but I know Tom is not okay. Shall we have some tea? Coffee? I have decaf."

"Decaf tea with milk would be great. I'll put on the kettle. Please tell me what's going on with Tom while you pull out the tea."

"Well, to be fair, Tom has had a lot on his plate since your dad died. You knew we'd need to hire help before harvest, but we're going to need help before then."

"Yeah. I knew that, I'll step up to do as much as possible, and I can probably be the second 'man' in the millroom at harvest."

"I've been trying to help out too, but I need direction. I've always been the best help when I don't try to figure out *how* to take care of the trees. Just give me a job and I'll do it. Tom says the voles are getting out of control. They're boring under the barrier tree trunks to make their nests and getting closer to the drip system. If we don't stop 'em soon, they'll kill the producing trees. The good news is, Tom says it looks like the olives will be larger this year and more of them. I know we need to place orders for containers, retail bottles, and labels. I can probably do that with some direction. Now that you're here, you can show me what I can do. "

"But, this is the slow time. Why hasn't Tom been keeping up? How come *he's* not giving you direction?"

Francesca squirmed in her chair, and then jumped when the kettle blasted its whistle.

Sherre twisted the knob on the range to silence it, and then turned to face her mom. Her mother's eyes looked anxious. "What is it? Is he sick?"

"You might say that. It doesn't seem to be completely out of control, but it's apparent that he's drinking again."

"Apparent? How?"

"I can smell it on his breath, even early in the morning. And his demeanor has changed. Moody. He gets so upset about little things. He throws mini-temper tantrums and blames anyone else in sight for whatever's wrong."

"Even you?"

Francesca's neck turned pink. "Um, yeah, even me. It's distressing. I think maybe he's angry that I've let Darian get so close so fast. Tom was so close to your dad. He's really more like a son than a son-in-law and your dad was the only dad Tom ever had. His mom raised him all by herself and did a great job, by the way. He always used to be so respectful." Francesca took a breath, and then a sip of her tea. "He's probably what counselors would call a 'working alcoholic,' though on occasion, he doesn't show up in the mornings. Once he was gone all day. Word is, he's been seen hanging out at the Garter Saloon."

"Oh." Sherre sat down. "Bummer." She pondered Deedee's insecurity about her weight. "We need more help than I thought. Has Deedee said anything to you?"

"No, but I don't see her all that often, like I used to before—"

Sherre nodded knowingly and felt her heart accelerate. "Before Darian, right?"

"Right." Francesca appeared to be wrestling with an interior struggle. "He's very nice to me, you know." A tentative smile lifted her face. "Your father never showered me with this kind of attention, even when we were dating."

Sherre said dryly, "Yeah. He's extraordinarily charming." She didn't add, *even to me*. His attention toward her had been unnerving. "Okay. We need to have a woman to woman talk to about Darian and your whirlwind romance soon, but not right now. First, we need to talk about the issues with the Ranch. You know that I want you to be happy, right? You don't need my approval—"

"Yeah. I kinda do, Sherre. As fun and exciting as this is, it's also scary for me."

Seeing distress cross her mother's face caused her to hurt in that place near her heart that had wrenched so often since she walked in on Chuck with Victoria. "I love you Mom." Sherre got up from the table and hugged Francesca around the back of her chair and held on as she said, "It's all going to work out. He seems like a nice guy," Sherre stepped back so she could see her mom's face, "but please try not to rush into anything, okay?"

Francesca nodded and fought her watery eyes. "It *is* moving very fast. I don't know much about this dating thing. When I married your dad, I was so young and naïve. I told Darian it was moving too fast for me and he's even been charming about that. But he keeps talking marriage and has from the start." She grinned. "I think he may be well off. Maybe if I marry him, he'll help us out of this financial mess."

Sherre shot her mom an incredulous look. "Yeah. That'll work. One of us can marry a rich man. I'll add the Cinderella scenario to my solutions matrix." Sherre sat back down and took a sip of her tea and smiled at her beautiful mother. They sat silently for a moment. "We need to work our problems out as capable, competent women, not like helpless Cinderellas. Let's start with the family we have now and talk about Darian another day." She massaged her temples for a moment. "Okay. I have a plan. First, I'll talk to Tom and see what's going on with him. I know he loves Deedee and the kids and would do anything for them. He's always been a hard worker and great to his family. He's got to know he's blowing it. What do you think happened? Do you think it was because Dad died?

"I'm not sure, but I think he may have picked up a bad habit before that. Your dad may have had something to do with it."

"What? Why?" Sherre felt her neck get red.

"You know your dad was so generous, and I don't think he ever took Tom's drinking problem seriously. His Italian heritage included daily wine with meals and he used to scoff at people who considered alcohol evil because throughout his family history, it never was. He didn't understand how it could get a hold of some people and ruin their lives. You know your dad always kept beer out in the millroom refrigerator, right?"

"No. When I helped with the milling, we didn't have that fancy, shmancy millroom and the new mill. We had to run the electricity to the barn to run the old mill and annually recreate the cleanroom, remember?"

"Oh yeah." Francesca shook her head. "So much has changed over the past five years."

"Well it doesn't matter what caused Tom's bad habit, what matters now is that he gets straightened out before he hurts Deedee and the kids or himself. Maybe if I have a talk with him he'll make the changes he needs to make. Or, maybe he'll need to go into a rehab facility. I don't know how we can get through harvest without him, but if he needs to go, we'll send him."

"And we'll have one more bill to pay."

"Yes, but Tom is family. Since great-great grandpa's time what's always been true about us Granzellas is we keep our heads up, make right decisions, and put family first."

Francesca smiled. "No wonder you're so good at what you do. I bet that positive attitude of yours can eclipse the bitter details of our crisis."

"Yeah, but the devil is in the details. I'll need to go over the accounting books."

"Take the laptop. It's in the front office."

Sherre looked intently at her mom and sighed. "I think you are all expecting a miracle from me. It's not like the Ranch has a lot of inefficiencies to fix, you know? I see my part in this is to find an influx of capital.

"And another thing. Deedee said you're not having Sunday dinners after church?"

Her mother shook her head slightly. "Not since you were here. We took a break after your dad—" Francesca's eyes glistened. "We never got back into our habit."

"We're back on this Sunday after church, okay? I'll pick up a nice piece of meat or poultry before Saturday and bake a pie or pick one up at Burgess." She grinned. Everyone knew Sherre loved pie.

Francesca returned the smile. "Good to have you back, Sherre."

CHAPTER FIVE

Surprise Help

After breakfast the next morning, Sherre sat at her grandfather's tiny, antique writing desk, and pushed the startup button on the Granzella laptop. While it was booting up, she explored the contents of the single, center drawer; a mere one and a half inches deep. In the front was a simple, gold ring, probably Grampa Bob's wedding ring. On each side of the ring sat a short stack of silver dollars. Directly behind these sat an emery board, a pen, and a pencil. Sherre tried out the pen on a yellowed, creased paper. It didn't work so she dropped it into the waste basket on the floor beside the desk. She unfolded the paper and noted that it was a room receipt from the Riverside Hotel on Virginia Street in Reno. She tapped each stack of silver dollars and smiled. An obstruction scraped as she tried to pull the drawer out further. She stuck her hand as far back she could, fishing around to find the source of resistance, but her fishing expedition was interrupted by a knock at her front door.

A tiny brunette with very stylish, short, wavy hair and large, brown eyes, stuck out her hand. "Hi. Kate Lockhart." It occurred to Sherre that the incredible length of Kate's eyelashes were disproportionate to her size, and yet Sherre knew they were real.

Sherre clasped Kate's strong grip, and said, "Hi Kate. How can I help you?" Sherre looked over Kate's shoulder and spotted a shiny, expertly detailed luxury vehicle parked next to her old car. She suspected it was a Bentley.

"Actually, I think I can help you. May I please come in?"

Sherre was suspicious, yet curious, "Sure," and waved her arm into the room. "How about some coffee or tea?"

"That would be lovely, but I just drove in from Stockton, I was wondering if I might—"

'Yes, of course. The bathroom is the second door." Sherre pointed to it, and then she pointed again to the larger door at the end of the room. "Meet me in the kitchen."

There were only two choices for entertaining. The rectangular box farmhouse had two main rooms. The room into which Kate entered was the entry room, living room, office, and oftentimes bedroom. Off to the right of the front door was the only actual bedroom. It had a second, connecting door to the bathroom. Sherre stood in the alcove at the low kitchen sink, filling the kettle with water. The sink had been constructed close to the floor to accommodate Sherre's reportedly, four-foot-eight great-grandmother, Adelina. Sherre looked passed the peeling paint of the kitchen window's wooden frame and chuckled to think that the kitchen sink was just about the right height for her tiny, expensively dressed, surprise visitor.

Sherre invited Kate to sit at the great, multiuse, wooden table that was the heart of the kitchen. The kitchen, of course, was the heart of the home.

"What a remarkable house!"

"Thanks. My great-grandfather built it, then it belonged to my grandfather, who was literally—" she paused and nodded, "—born here. Then it was my parents before they moved into the new house up on the hill. Now it's going to be mine for a while." She winced, realizing how brief a time that that might be.

"Am I right that when I was walking to your front door on the porch, then from the living room to the kitchen that I was walking uphill?"

Sherre giggled. "Yup. That section of the house is built over a crawl space. I think the amateur family builders sort of followed the lay of the land rather than a level when they laid the foundation. Or to be fair, it could have settled. This house is almost a hundred years old. The living room carpet is new to our generation. At holiday and birthday celebrations, my Grandpa Bob used to seat my sister and me at the low end of the room and roll silver dollars to us on the wooden floor."

"Wow! Silver dollars? I haven't see one of those for a while."

"Grandpa Bob was quite the fan of dollar slot machines. He made regular trips to Reno. It's only a couple of hours from here."

"I love that old claw-foot bathtub." She nodded toward the bathroom. "And your wood stoves." Kate pointed behind Sherre to the full-sized cast iron stove seated alongside the modern gas range. "Is that stove, and the potbelly in the living room, the only source of heat?"

"Yep. In the winter, we keep that door between the two main rooms closed. Once the living room fire dies down, we build a new fire to light after sundown. When this one dies down, we get it ready to light in the chilly morning. In the summer, it's hot. Look," Sherre pointed to the painted tongue and groove wall between the back kitchen door and the window. "Can you see daylight coming through that crack? Windy nights tend to be drafty in here. There are gaps like that throughout the house."

Kate looked up toward the naked bulb hanging on a twisted wire from the ceiling. "But you have electricity."

"Yeah. Though the heating system is primitive, the electrical wiring was upgraded in the fifties to adapt to a changing lifestyle that included a TV and a vacuum cleaner." She scoffed. "We still blow fuses if we stress the resources. In fact, my sister and her kids just cleaned this old place up for me. She told me that when she was ready to vacuum, she unplugged the refrigerator just in case." Pointing to the gas stove, "A propane tank supplies that as well as the hot water heater that's around that wall. The kitchen sink and refrigerator are also in that alcove. Before electricity, my grandparents had an ice box and they used the cellar as a larder. It's below a portion of this room. Pretty small. Only about a quarter of the room."

"Wow. Cool house. Great history."

Sherre chuckled, "Yeah. I never got the story straight regarding my great-grandfather, Maurizio Granzella. When he landed in San Francisco, he was either nineteen with twenty-one dollars in his pocket or twenty-one with nineteen dollars. At great risk to himself and his family in Italy, he protected and hid an American soldier during World War I. The soldier offered to help Grandpa Maurizio start a new life in America if he would come to the West Coast after the War. Grandpa Maurizio met my grandma, Adelina Russo, and her family at the San Francisco immigration office. He married her two months later and moved out to here to the Sierra foothills.

"So Kate, what brings you to Granzella Ranch and what makes you think you can help me? Are you selling something?"

"Oh no. I'm not selling anything." She shook her head. "I'm writing a book, or booklet really, for the Olive Oil Council and I know absolutely nothing about the olive oil business." She blew some steam off the top of her tea cup. "Marilyn Hofstadter, on the council, recommended that I contact you. She said your family probably knows more about the business than anyone, and that maybe you'd even let me rent one of your cabins for a few weeks until you need it for harvest. I'd like to work for you while I'm here. I don't suppose you could use a neophyte assistant that requires training?"

"Um. Wow. Yeah, actually we sure could use some help, but, well—"

"You don't have to pay me. Does that help?"

"Of course, but that's not right."

"Sure it is. It's not really advantageous for me to make money. It only creates a higher tax liability and is therefore a nuisance."

Sherre felt as if envy had crept in through one of the airy crevices in the wall panels. "Must be nice. Oh! Kate Lockhart, as in Horace Lockhart Publishing?"

"Yes."

"I always wondered what independently wealthy people did with most of their time."

Kate smiled. "They write books and work for free. There is one thing I would ask from you, however—"

"What's that?"

"If you introduce me to anyone or need to refer to me in any way, please only use my nom de plume, the one I gave the Olive Oil Council, Kate Stryker."

"Okay. Why didn't you just give *me* your nom de plume?"

"I'm not sure. It's an integrity issue I think. I actually planned on introducing myself as Kate Stryker, but when I got to your door, I just couldn't do it, asking you to let me live and work here. Not right." She shook her head. "Not right." She reiterated. "I needed to tell you who I really am."

"Stryker," Sherre looked up at the ceiling. "Didn't I see that name somewhere recently?"

"Yes. You saw it on my license plate when you looked over my shoulder at my car. I changed my personalized plate to STRYKER."

CHAPTER SIX

Kate

Kate Lockhart had an ulterior motive for manipulating her way into the workings of Granzella Ranch. She wanted to personally keep an eye on Darian Danville. She had hired a private investigator to investigate him after her own mother's death. She grew suspicious when he began courting the Granzella Ranch matriarch.

Kate's grandfather, Horace Lockhart, attended the University of Maryland and graduated magna cum laude, and then he continued his education at Harvard Law School. He established himself in a successful law practice in St. Louis, Missouri, but he was fascinated by newspapers and their ability, in his view, to shape and improve a community. He bought a small newspaper in a suburb of St.

Louis, but was unable to generate revenue. Shortly after World War II, he moved to California and purchased a slightly larger newspaper in Stockton, renaming it the Stockton Life and Times. The local economy was emerging after the World War II, particularly with babies being born everywhere, including hospital corridors, because there were not enough delivery rooms to accommodate them. Lockhart saw the baby boom as a vehicle for advertising revenues. He invited some prominent local business owners to dinner and asked them to advertise, thus solidifying the paper's financial position. By 1970, with more than a dozen small papers scattered across three counties, Horace Lockhart was the fourth richest man in California. He educated, cultivated, and indoctrinated his only son, Horace Lockhart Jr., into his newspaper empire before bequeathing it to him.

Horace Jr. was a workaholic and what everyone considered a hopeless bachelor until, at the age of sixty seven, he met Julianna Dion, a lovely public relations consultant for Hilton Enterprises.

Julianna was only thirty-five and felt very much alone in this world. She'd been raised in the foster system, futilely waiting for her mother to return for her. The final set of foster parents encouraged her to start community college while still in high school. Julianna's excellent grades opened scholarships to the University system. After graduating with a degree in Media Communications, she landed her job at Hilton. Her career became her new family. When Julianna met Horace Lockhart Jr., she was captivated by this formidable, influential man. She felt judged by gossip and resisted three marriage proposals before giving in. For in fact, Julianna had fallen in love, not with Horace's fortune and generosity as everyone believed, but rather with his kind underlying nature that was rarely revealed to others. His love for her filled the chasm of loneliness she'd known all her life. They married in nineteen-ninety-one and had Kathrine Julianna Lockhart in December of ninety-two.

Kate was a loved, bright child who excelled as a student. Her parents enrolled her in private schools that permitted her to live at home. The family's wealth far exceeded that of other families in Kate's schools, which caused Kate to question the sincerity of her few friendships, especially of would-be suitors. However, when Whelan Duval started walking her to class and patiently drawing her out of her shell, she quit fighting her emotions. She felt excitement each time he called. Each night when she laid her head on her pillow, she obsessively replayed every encounter and conversation with him earlier in the day. Whelan invited her to the Senior Ball and she accepted.

Julianna and Kate enthusiastically went shopping to find the perfect dress. Kate took dancing lessons. Horace Jr. determined to vet this stranger that dared to date his daughter. The young man came from a good family, with pedigrees of sorts. They owned a large mansion near the elite Brookside Country club. Inquiry revealed that Whelan's parents had inherited a small fortune from Whelan's maternal grandmother, but had lost most of it through impudent ventures and flipping houses. Before the Ball, Horace Jr. took Whelan aside in the study and warned the young man that if he was trifling with his daughter's heart to regain his family's wealth, there was something that he needed to know. The Lockhart fortune was in a living trust that belonged to Horace Jr., his wife Julianna, and his daughter, Kate. If his daughter married or his wife remarried after his death, their husbands would have zero access to the trust.

At the Ball, Kate relaxed dreamily into Whelan's arms as they danced. She had the sensation that everyone else in the room was seeing them as a couple. Until that moment she hadn't realized how without him, she had felt so lonely and invisible in the story of her own life.

She could feel his heart beating through his tux as he tenderly held her close. She heard him breathing quietly and pictured, in the dark shadows of the dance floor, that his eyes were closed as his face rested against the top of her head.

They talked and laughed as if this magical evening had been created for them alone. He held her hand throughout the evening, occasionally bringing it to his lips. It seemed to Kate that there was a sense of desperation in the way he kissed her repeatedly in the backseat of the stretch limo on the ride home. At Kate's front door, he kissed her one last time. She looked up and felt confident to say, "Will you call me tomorrow?"

He jerked his head, laughed, a false, hard sound and said, "No."

She pushed him away so she could look in his eyes, and then asked incredulously, "No?"

"No. Sorry, but this won't work for me. I thought it might, but your dad made it clear when the evening started, that this is not what I thought I was getting into." He turned on his heel and coiled to the limo.

She felt heat blistering her cheeks. She was so confused. *What could her father have possibly said?* She wondered how a man could pretend to be so amorous and passionately kiss a girl goodnight, all the while intending to never see her again.

And he never did see her again.

The night of Kate's Senior Ball was the last night of her father's life. She burst into his bedroom with hot angry tears planning to scream at him and insist that he tell her what he'd said to Whelan, but her forward motion, her tears, and her anger halted abruptly at the sight of her mother sitting beside him, holding his hand, weeping silently.

Hot tingles shot through Kate's arms and fingers; even her nose and chin were tingling. "Oh Daddy!" She rushed to the other side of his bed and took his other hand. This side of his face looked as if it were made of wax that was melting, but there was life in his eyes; a clamor of emotion pent up that he was unable to convey.

The doctor arrived moments later, but there was no need for him to examine Horace Jr., merely for him to confirm what they already knew. The two women he loved dearly each held a hand that had gone entirely cold.

Before retiring several years before, Horace Jr. had sold all of his holdings. When he died, the trust he left his wife and daughter was valued close to a half of a billion dollars.

Julianna and Kate went through all the necessary motions of burying, securing copies of his death certificate, crossing all the legal and proper T's and dotting all the inevitable i's. They were the only family they had and they felt no need or desire to bring the public into their grieving ritual.

Several days later, Julianna peered over her morning coffee at her daughter and said, "How was the Senior Ball?" The resulting conversation lead to Kate bowing out of the last days and ceremonies of high school. She had far exceeded graduation requirements before the Ball and she had no desire to march in a diploma assembly with Whelan. Nor did she feel up to delivering her Valedictorian speech. When she talked to her counselor she said, "Give someone else a chance. And look at the bright side, now you don't need to find a box for me to stand on."

Kate argued that Julianna should not be alone, but her mother insisted that Kate continue with her plans to study abroad for one year.

Kate's father's death was not as shocking as her mother's.

The first month after Horace and Kate were gone from Julianna's life, she found herself preoccupied with acute loneliness. The second month, a handsome, ostensibly successful, real estate agent, Darian Danville began to lavish romantic attention on the fifty-seven year old widow. Julianna lost her sense of balance. She was a stylish, lovely woman who looked at least ten years younger than her age. It wasn't out of the question that this dapper, thirty-five year old was sincerely captivated by her attractiveness. Kate got a call from her mother four months later. She'd accepted Darian's proposal of marriage. Six months after the death of her father, Darian and her mother eloped before Kate could offer to take a break from school.

Julianna asked Darian what he would like as a wedding present and bought him a Moomba Outback ski boat. He towed the boat behind a rented motorhome and took his new bride camping at Lake Shasta. The first morning on the lake, Darian called 911 at five AM. He wanted to report a missing person. He said his wife and he had gone to bed at ten thirty after they had drunk a whole bottle of champagne.

When he awoke at three-thirty, his wife and his boat were gone.

Sheriff's deputies called in investigators and a search-and-rescue team. Huge cumulous clouds were blowing in and yet the sun, as though in contest, shot between the billowing clouds. They checked at nearby marinas, but there was no sign of Julianna. A helicopter was brought in. Portions of the water sparkled with frenzied glory and other portions were covered in gloomy darkness where the huge clouds blocked the sun. The blazing glare and uneven patches of light inhibited their search beneath the water, but a few minutes after eight AM, they spotted the jet boat, resting against the shore two and a half miles from the Danville campsite. On the boat's seat, deputies found the T-shirt Juliana had gone to sleep in. On the floor were her blue jeans. Low-flying helicopters crisscrossed the lake basin to no avail. Then, just before four, a radio call came from the news helicopter operated by Channel 3, the local NBC affiliate. With assistance of shade from one of the puffy clouds, they'd spotted something. Within minutes, divers were in the water. There, in eight feet of water, twenty feet from shore, on the muddy lake bottom, they found the body of Julianna Lockhart Danville, clad only in bra and panties.

By the time the authorities reached Kate, they had ruled her mother's death an accidental drowning. There was only a slight abrasion on her forehead, where Julianna's body had presumably bumped against the lake bottom after a shallow dive. There were no unexplainable bruises or wounds. Additionally, her blood-alcohol concentration was .08%, the minimum legal level to be considered drunk.

Kate believed otherwise. She deliberately stayed in Belgium, staying in touch with her attorney, asking him to handle all local arrangements. She asked her lawyer to tell her stepfather, whom she'd never met, that she had final tests and would not be returning home. As with her father's passing, since there was no one else with whom she cared to share her grief, she chose not to hold a funeral or memorial service. Kate conscientiously determined that Darian Danville would not recognize her if they were to meet. She was convinced he was too self-absorbed to have studied pictures of her. She wanted the freedom to observe his behavior in person when she returned to the States. Regardless of the ruling, she was certain her mother's death was no accident. She was certain Darian Danville murdered her mother for her money. There was enough community property for him to score about two million if he would sell the home they'd moved into, the vehicles, the boat, and the furniture, but he would soon taste a bitter pill of knowledge: The enormous Lockhart estate was safely secured in a trust unavailable to him.

Kate waited almost a year before she returned to California to set in motion a comprehensive investigation into this slick, charming suitor. She began by setting up a meeting with the lead detective in her mother's accident, Detective Anthony West, of the Shasta Sheriff's Department.

"I'm so sorry for your loss. Believe me, we searched for evidence. Nothing felt right, but in the end, we couldn't prove your mother's death was anything but an accident. However, I've kept the investigation open."

Kate's private detective agency discovered that Julianna's mysterious death was not the only death from which he'd benefitted. Darian Danville was the only child of parents who died in an airplane accident when he was nearing high school graduation. Kate realized, of course, that he had nothing to do with that tragedy, but she wondered if his first inheritance instilled in him a greedy, no-need-to-work ethic. He graduated from high school, but didn't pursue higher education. For several years he lived off his parent's dwindling bank accounts and their life insurance payout in their comfortable home in an upscale Stockton suburb. Credit reports indicated he needed to start generating income. He worked hard to get a real estate license, but did not work as hard at real estate. Instead, he used his market listings as a network to find single, wealthy women. After several failed attempts, he found Dolly Martin, an unattractive, but extremely wealthy divorcée. He moved in with her and rented out his parent's home. A wedding date was set for shortly after her alimony checks would cease. But, when Darian heard that Horace Jr.'s lovely widow, Julianna Lockhart was available, he dumped Dolly and broke her heart.

After Julianna's death, Darian attained another source of income that supplemented his Lockhart inheritance. Kate's investigators weren't sure if consistent deposits into Darian's accounts from his well-to-do, widowed, maternal grandmother were due to his manipulation of her, or possibly misappropriation of the funds that he was managing for her, but the vilest suspicious evidence was almost too cruel and sociopathic to consider. Nine months before Kate started her investigation, his grandmother died in an automobile accident. Darian was her sole heir. His grandmother ran a stop sign at the bottom of a steep incline and T-boned a truck. The driver, Rob Granzella, died at the scene also. Police reports detailed Darian Danville's behavior when he showed up at the crash scene. With a great deal of drama and morose explanation, he proclaimed to the police how it was all his fault. He should have insisted that his grandmother stop driving after she accidentally hit the gas pedal instead of the brake pedal and drove through the back of her own garage. Kate's investigators said the grandmother's accident with Rob Granzella was handled as just that. Darian's grandmother was getting old and Darian had apparently persuaded them that her faculties were failing. No one examined the brakes of his grandmother's car to see if they'd been tampered with or checked to see if, indeed, the garage at his grandmother's house was recently damaged. Kate's investigators also determined that Darian had most likely met Francesca Granzella for the first time at her husband's funeral and that he was now spending a great deal of time at her olive oil ranch.

Kate's heart ached with loss and regret. She missed her mother and her father. In the midnight hours, she repeatedly replayed the past. She rewrote her part in the story to produce a different end. In the do-over, instead of studying abroad, Kate stayed home with her mom as a wise counselor who warned her not to fall into the clutches of the handsome, sociopathic sleazeball. Kate's small comfort was that Darian Danville hadn't acquired the entire Lockhart fortune, but it was a small consolation. The hurt wouldn't go away, so she tried to get used to it by moving forward with a plan. *Get close to this despicable man and try to protect his next innocent victim.* If she was totally honest with herself, she would confess that she also wanted revenge.

CHAPTER SEVEN

Work

It was a good problem to have. Sherre hoped that Tom would show up at the millroom early and he did, but she was unable to have the heart to heart talk with him she'd rehearsed throughout her virtually sleepless night. Kate showed up early as well, and Sherre would never think it was a problem to have Kate. She was still tempted to pinch herself to make sure she hadn't dreamed that this wonderful woman offered to help out right when they needed it. As soon as Kate left the previous day, Sherre enlisted her sister and the kids to help turnout, clean, and disinfect the fifth wheel's interior. They also gave the outside a wash. It had nicer amenities than the cabins, but Sherre kept thinking, *not nice enough for a millionaire heiress.* They cleared two parking places in the old barn, one spot for Sherre's car which was Grandma Dorothy's eighty-six BMW, and one spot for Kate's Bentley. Their personal plates were a remarkable side by side, FIXER and STRYKER.

"Kate, this is my brother-in-law, Tom March. Tom, this is Kate Stryker. She wants to learn about the olive oil business and work for us as she learns." Sherre studied Tom's appearance as he shook Kate's hand, and waited for them to exchange pleasantries before she stepped forward to give him a sideways hug and a peck on the cheek. "Hi Bro." He'd gained some weight in the past nine months. His face was puffy. His eyes were rimmed with red.

"Hi Tom." Kate shook Tom's hand in her forceful, professional way. "So, what a nice millroom."

"In Italian, it's the Frantio."

Kate pulled her phone out of her pocket and started taking notes. "Frantio? F-R-A-N-T-I-O, right?"

Sherre nodded. "You're good."

"I love Italian. It's so predictable."

"We extract the oil within hours of harvest with that state-of-the-art, Pieralisi olive mill. We also mill small batches for many of our neighbors throughout the harvest. Those are called fusties." Sherre pointed to a gleaming row of stainless steel containers with pouring spigots.

Kate spoke some of her notes into her phone, typed in the words that autocorrect would massacre, and then stuffed her phone back into the front pocket of her jeans. She directed her statement and question to Tom, not Sherre, "So put us to work. What can we do today?"

Tom's cheeks flushed. He was obviously pleased with Kate's support, Sherre's loving greeting, and finding he was still in charge. "It's kill week." He expected a more dramatic response, but they both nodded determinedly.

"First, I need to run you both through some mandatory training. I have a Private Applicator License for bait and organic pesticide usage. As long as I go over all of these rules and regulations regarding entry restrictions, application limitations, postings, oral warnings, pesticide use information, and protection from employer retaliation," he smiled at Sherre, "I can send you out to kill along the barrier trees. Are you sure you're up for this?"

Kate said, "Sure. I'll do whatever you need me to do." She pulled out her phone to take more notes. "What are barrier trees?"

"We have a few rows of trees that we don't harvest—we knock the fruit off of them so they don't attract fruit flies. Then we destroy or bury all the perimeter fruit. We keep critters at bay in the barrier trees by approved standard farming methods. But, the trees inside the barrier—the ones that we harvest—we strictly adhere to certified organic procedures."

Sherre turned to Kate, "It's a horrible job, but if we don't do this, we'll diminish our olive harvest and lose many of the trees. These little rodents, called voles, build their nests in the base of the trees and then breed like, well, rodents. They not only expose roots, they gnaw on our drip irrigation system, chewing holes with their sharp, pointy teeth." She wrinkled her nose and wiggled two fingers like fangs in front of her mouth.

"I'm ahead of the game." Tom picked up a white plastic pipe that was elbowed at one end and had another pipe protruding at a right angle out of its middle. "This is a bait station." Two weeks ago, I placed a bunch of these along the outer perimeter of the barrier trees—did Sherre tell you we have an adjacent neighbor with unattended walnut and almond orchards? Yeah? Last week I filled the bait stations with untainted oatmeal so the destructive little buggers would begin to trust the food source. "They crawl in through here. These covers keep larger animals, like kit foxes or, God forbid someone's little curious dog, from getting to the poison. Now, it's time to fill the bait traps with oatmeal laced with poison." He smirked.

"What? What's with that mischievous grin?"

"After you guys finish filling the bait traps I have another job for you."

"Ew. Don't tell me, let me guess. Is it sticky and stinky? I don't think we should ask Kate to do that."

"Do what?"

"Yeah, Sherre's right. We shouldn't ask you to check the yeast traps. We have a certified organic spray, but it's incredibly expensive so we put out traps with a yeast mixture in them to attract any fruit flies in the area, then we only spray in the sections that do."

Sherre wrinkled her nose. "It's amazingly disgusting. Plus it's challenging. It's hard to see the tiny insects. First-timers need a magnifying glass. Then, you need to hover over the stinky trays to count the flies. They cluster in certain areas of the orchards. This is how we know which sections need spray."

Tom felt conflicted as he watched them head down the hill with sacks of bait in the bed of the farm's truck. When they were reasonably out of sight, he opened the refrigerator. *Just one beer. Hair of the dog.*

Halfway through the day, Sherre called Kate. "Break time. Let's go get lunch. Meet me at my mom's. She said she'd prepare something."

They met up in the orchard, heading in the same direction. "Gosh. I've been noticing all day how quiet it is out here, but now, what's that hammering noise?"

"Sounds like it's coming from my house." They picked up their pace.

Johnny's truck was backed up to the kitchen-end of Sherre's house. The wobbly staircase that Sherre descended this morning had disappeared. The kitchen door hovered above a half-story drop. Next to the truck was a pile of discarded wood. In the bed of Johnny's truck was a load of clean, new lumber. Johnny was pounding on one of six posts he'd strategically placed to support a new staircase and landing. He turned to see both women petting Marcus, the welcoming committee.

Kate said, "Wow, who's that? He looks a lot like—"

"Yeah, I know and his name is Johnny, Johnny *Banks*. This is his dog, Marcus." They reached the house. "Johnny, you are so sweet. Just this morning, I was wondering when that landing and staircase would give way. It felt so unstable, before I got to the bottom stair, I decided to exclusively use the living room front door, even if I was headed up to Mom's or needed to go down to the cellar." She pointed to the exposed cellar doorway beneath the house. "I was thinking about asking you a favor."

"I wish you would." One side of Johnny's mouth turned up.

"Now I don't have to."

"Now you don't have to." He repeated matter-of-factly, and then smiled. "I'm going to rebuild the other stairs too, after I give this entrance back to you."

"Like you've got nothing else to do, right?"

"Right, and you should see how much lumber is leftover in Dad's storehouse. He'd be pleased that I'm using some of it up this way."

"Oh, Sorry. Kate Stryker, this is Johnny Banks." They exchanged courteous nods and Sherre noticed Kate discretely examining frame and form that was Johnny. "Kate's working alongside of me to learn more about the olive oil business. She's writing a booklet for the California Olive Oil Council. Want some lunch? Mom said she'd have something ready for us. Tom's coming down too."

"I'll pass. My mom thinks I'm too thin. You should've seen the breakfast she fed me this morning. It'll last at least 'til dinner, maybe until tomorrow." He chuckled a brief machinegun outburst. "Besides. I need to keep going." He lifted his eyebrows, then looked down at the black plastic barrel mixer at his feet that resembled a small beer keg. "Wet cement."

Sherre's chin jerked when her front jean's pocket sounded a ding. "Uh oh. That's my lawyer's ringtone. Will you excuse me?" She wandered up the hill toward her mother's house. Johnny and Kate watched as Sherre did more nodding than talking into her phone. Then she slipped her phone back into her pocket and signaled to Kate to follow.

"You okay?"

"Yeah, but I don't need this right now." Sherre felt overwhelmed like she'd been hit with a fist to her chest. She decided to confide in Kate. "I'm going through a divorce. I make a lot more than my husband and—"

"And he wants alimony, right?"

"Yes."

"Ah yes, the double-edged sword of feminism. I'm sorry."

"Yeah. Good grief! He moved back into our house that I pretty much paid for. Now he wants more money from me so he can afford to stay in it. I'm beginning to think I've never met anyone as slow witted as I am. I have so many regrets. I keep asking myself why I didn't know better when the signs were so obvious all along. You know what?" She chuckled. "This is not what you came to learn. Sorry to dump my personal problems on you like this."

"No. Really. It's all good." Behind her eyes swirled some inexplicable anxiety and sadness. "I, um, well. I'm not sure how else to say this, but yesterday, when we met, I sort of thought we'd become friends."

Sherre felt a sudden flood of delight and studied Kate's face for a minute as she considered her words. She also had felt a deep-seated connection with Kate. It was as if they had more in common than what was apparent on the surface. "I think you're right." She smiled broadly. "Isn't this terrific? You came here without knowing us and we have this unexplainable connection. I feel like I've known you for a very long time."

"Yes. I feel that way too."

"I actually have very few friends. My best friends are my mom and my sister—Oh what a dunderhead!" Sherre slapped her forehead. "I'm sorry. I read about your mom."

"Yeah." Kate looked down at the ground as they hiked toward the Granzella farmhouse. "She *was* my best friend. But please don't apologize. It's okay. I'm glad you have your mom and your sister, and nothing, including pretending that it didn't happen, will bring my mom back. Trust me. I've tried that."

Sherre was having difficulty forgiving herself for saying something so insensitive. They continued on their way in silence, listening only to Johnny's hammering and the sound of their shoes crunching on the gravel driveway beneath them. She remembered the story of Kate's mom on the news and thought at the time that the accidental death sounded suspicious. Sherre assumed the newly-wed husband inherited the vast fortune and wondered where he had gone. And now she was walking up the hill to her mother's home with the heiress who had lost so much. "I really am so sorry for your loss. I—I, okay, I won't apologize again, but I want to. It's so hard to lose a parent. My dad died last year. In fact, he was on his way to visit me after he finally had a day off after the last harvest. The worst, of course, was that we lost him as father and husband, but it was also a devastating loss to our business. He bought out his brother after my grandpa died, so he was Granzella Ranch's sole administrator and manager, as well as our most experienced worker. And, we not only lost him, we lost a valuable piece of our farming equipment. He was driving his truck, which was totaled in the accident that killed him." Sherre was forced to stop talking as her emotions rose to close her throat and cloud her eyes.

Kate reached over to pat Sherre's forearm. "I know."

Sherre nodded, realizing that her friend understood, perhaps better than anyone outside of her family ever had. She lifted her hand beneath one eye, and then the other to wipe away the tears.

Darian's Cadillac was not around so they mounted the steps, tapped, and walked through the ranch house front door. Sherre hugged her mother and enjoyed the lingering scent of morning soaps and cosmetics. "Kate, this is my mom, Francesca Granzella. Mom, Kate Stryker. Where's Tom?"

Francesca tucked her lips into each other tightly for a second, and the she let out a breath, not far from a sigh, "He called. Said he wouldn't be here. Didn't tell me why."

Kate interrupted the uneasy silence, "Well it certainly is kind of you to feed me. I didn't expect this."

"Of course, of course. As long as you're staying here we'll consider you family. In fact, we'd love you to come to lunch after church on Sunday, that's if you don't have other plans."

"Um, well, no. I was just going to stay in the trailer and write. That would be lovely.

What smells so delicious?"

Sherre said, "That's Mom's butternut squash soup."

"Do you treat all your farm workers like this?" Kate tilted her head and raised one perfectly-shaped eyebrow.

Francesca put her hand on the top of Kate's shoulder. "We feed them lunch, but not in the house and we don't invite them to Sunday dinner."

"I feel special."

"I'd say you're special," said Sherre. "I'm still amazed that you showed up at this most opportune moment."

Sherre heard the front and screen doors wheeze open and slam shut. Her mind questioned that Deedee would come to Mom's in the middle of the day, and then she turned to see Darian make his entrance across the wooden floor, which glowed like honey where the sun was splayed across it. She thought, *Golden Boy waltzing across a golden floor.*

His gaze zoomed directly to Kate. "Well hello." His eyes squinted as he tilted his head. "Have we met?" He stuck his hand out. "Darian Danville."

"Kate Stryker." She nodded and refused his gesture. Her extraordinarily, long eye lashes touched her eyebrows as she returned a deliberate gaze. "No. I'm positive we've never met."

Darian's face twitched at the refusal of his hand, but he quickly recovered his pompous attitude, and then put his arm around Francesca before kissing her on the cheek. "Hi Beautiful."

"Hi. Have you had lunch?"

"No. Seems I have good timing."

Sherre's phone buzzed in the front of her jeans. She looked at it and said, "It's Denny Garter." She waved her hand backward as she walked toward the front door. "Please start without me. Hi Denny." She stepped out to the front porch and dropped into her favorite wicker chair. "Long time, no see."

"Yeah. And you're not seeing me now. How about dinner tonight?"

"Sure. At your saloon?"

"No. I'll take you to Theresa's in Jackson. Somewhere you can dress up pretty if you want."

"Er, well okay."

"I'll pick you up at 7:00? You're at your granddad's house, right?"

CHAPTER EIGHT

Denny

Dennis Garter stood sideways in front of the full-length mirror on his bedroom closet door, sucked in his stomach, and then pressed it in further with the palms of his large hands. He probably weighed only slightly more than he did when he played football in high school, but his athletic body had mislaid its athleticism. The previously mighty muscles of his arms and chest had seemingly melted into his belly region. He kept examining himself, straining to predict how Sherre Granzella would see him on their dinner date. He was used to being the shortest man in the room as he had been the shortest man on the football team, but his speed had given him glory as a receiver. After his football glory days, he capitalized on his superior intellect, business acumen, and a princely face that charmed acceptance from women and potential business partners. He had a strong jaw and thick, dark eyelashes that commanded attention. His dark wavy hair was getting white at the temples. She'd find that distinguished. *She was still such a fox.*

When he attended her father's memorial he wasn't sure she'd seen him. The entire county showed up and he didn't fight for her attention. Now that he heard she had left Chuck, he wished he had found a way to be more noticeable to her. He was sure, however, that she knew Wanda had left him for another man, leaving him with sole responsibility of Tyler, now thirteen. Everyone knew. He winced at his reflection. The only regret he had toward Wanda though was that he probably spoiled her. He was loyal, kind, and patient with her. Throughout his life he had observed his father's generosity toward his mother and recognized this as the secret to a happy marriage. It wasn't surprising that when she departed, she left Tyler behind. He deeply loved the boy and Wanda knew it. Pangs of sadness felt dark and trembling in his chest. *Cuckold, the greatest offense.* His thoughts wandered onto a familiar train. *Insulting and embarrassing, not just to me, but to the boy that came with her into our marriage. Maybe I can turn this to an advantage with Sherre. Seems like she'd be a gal who wished she had children by now.*

Denny intentionally, often aggressively, controlled most conversations. He strived to be an expert on pretty much everything and considered it a license to direct others with his expertise. He instructed them where they should go on vacation and what they should do there. When friends expressed a need for something, he readily advised them what they should buy, where they should go to buy it, and specifically how to use his recommendations. His parents, and select teachers knew he started life with a far above average IQ. His over-active brain inspired his insatiable curiosity and filled him with enthusiasm. He often interrupted others before they finished talking. While driving his late model, top of the line Dodge RAM pickup, he listened to podcasts on his phone. He devoured knowledge on the Internet daily. He was ofttimes aware that his constant talking and poor listening skills revealed a deep-seated loneliness. He would try to be a better listener tonight.

He donned his newly purchased, black, Armani jeans and T-shirt. He obscured his protruding belly with his black, Domenico Vacca sports coat—all from a recent trip to Neiman Marcus in San Francisco. He strutted in front of the mirror again, deciding whether to wear his Stetson. He thought not. *Need to look humble.*

"Whoa, Dad! A jacket? Did someone die?"

"Hey Tyler. No death. I've got a date." He sought approval from his scrawny son, feeling slightly ashamed of his previous, mean dispiritedness toward Tyler earlier in the day. Denny had managed, as he intended, to get Tyler upset, but it didn't accomplish what Denny had hoped. Denny regularly used humiliating techniques hoping the boy would see Denny's disappointment and desire to change, but only the first part stuck. It seemed his parenting skills had a default state of regretful. It was just the degree of regret that changed. The boy probably hated himself. Denny resented that the kid was so thin, wouldn't eat wholesome food, and only had passion for video games, but he had no idea how to motivate him. He desired the best for Tyler in every way, but he couldn't seem to rise above the frustrations of parenting. While trying to control this uncontrollable kid, he continued to blame Wanda, though she had been gone for several years now. He needed a new wife. A good wife. Tyler needed a mother. A good mother. He hoped he could persuade foxy Sherre into taking this open position. She was known as the Fixer. He would try to convince her that she could fix Tyler.

A smile glimmered on the lower half of Tyler's face. It was such a rare occurrence, it startled a smile onto to Denny's face too. "You know your friend, Courtney? I've asked her Aunt Sherre, out for dinner tonight."

"Courtney says her Aunt Sherre is going to fix things. I don't understand. You know how Courtney is. She says stuff that's way out there sometimes."

"You know Courtney better than I do, but she sure seems like a brainiac. Her Aunt

Sherre's got a reputation for taking companies that don't work and not only getting them to work, but also start making money. But, she's not going to be able to do it with her family's ranch."

"Why not?"

"Because it's not broken, it's just broke." He felt amused by his own cleverness.

"So, will Courtney have to move?"

Denny lifted his eyebrows. "If I didn't know better, I'd think you are sweet on her. An older woman?"

Tyler shot back with an accusing tone, "Mom is five years older than you."

Denny recognized, as he often did, an opportunity to manipulate this situation to his advantage. "What would you think if your old man was trying to save Courtney's family from having to move?" He squinted his eyes and nodded his head.

"Really. It won't be Courtney's parents who make the decision though. It'll be Sherre. She'll be the one to call the shots. That's why I'm taking her out to dinner—

Wish me luck."

CHAPTER NINE

Tyler

If Tyler didn't guard his feelings in the real world, he would recognize that he actually was, as his dad proposed, sweet on Courtney. She fascinated him. Everything was so literal and precise with her. She reminded him of his computer and he *loved* his computer.

Destiny was his game of choice. It created the world in which he preferred to live. His story in that world was more compelling than the story of his ordinary life. In the world of Destiny, he was a winner, but in the stark reality of school he was often viewed as a loser, even by himself. His video game experiences made him feel like he was part of something bigger than himself. In his Destiny fantasy world, he was not Denny Garter's disappointing son, nor Wanda's abandoned boy, nor even dull, ordinary Tyler. In Destiny, he was Crusader_5-0; a Titan and a defender. He was part of an adroit fireteam that struck against the forces of Darkness. He defended his teammates in raids. They relied on him to protect them. He liked that.

Tyler tried sometimes to be a hero to his mother in the real world, but he couldn't seem to gain her love. She called once in a while and convinced him she'd come visit him if he would send her enough money for train fare. The last time seemed like about twenty-thousand trains ago. He recently resigned himself to the reality that she'd never come.

He hoped his dad could help Courtney's family so she wouldn't move. She was the only one whom he had never heard mocking him behind his back. Even when he didn't hear them, he felt their revulsion and saw their eyes roll when he gave answers in class. It was a subtle kind of bullying. The subtlety arose from an early grasp of politics. The junior high school set had begun to understand the power of money and they knew Tyler's dad controlled most of it in the Calaveras school district. Most of his classmates were clueless that he was their champion, Crusader_5-0. However, Courtney's little brother, Tommy, also known as "Mighty_Midas07," did know Tyler's Destiny screen name. Tommy also got the Five-O reference to law enforcement. Tommy practically worshipped Tyler. It felt good that someone looked up to him, even though the hero worship was grounded in a video game. One more reason why Tyler wanted the family to stay.

CHAPTER TEN

It's Not Just Dinner

Sherre was ready early for her date with Denny so she sat down at her grandfather's desk and opened the Granzella laptop. She felt an unbearable apprehension, but she wasn't sure of its source. She was unaccustomed to failure and hadn't reconciled her mind to the possibility that she might fail at the most important fix ever. Everyone was counting on her for a miracle, but that would be in God's wheelhouse, not hers. Her battle plans included analysis, strategy and contingency. The analysis was complete, but in the true spirit of denial, she opened her projected budget spreadsheet to try again. She was increasingly convinced that any efforts to make adjustments to where to spend time, money, and energy would be futile. She felt a deep twinge in her abdomen as she admitted to herself she may need to change her goal. Rather than save the Ranch, she'd need to make a different plan—possibly make a deal with Denny Garter—that insured her family's financial security. She felt a snag on a fingernail and thought she remembered seeing an emery board, so she pulled the handle on the little drawer. A scrape reminded her that something was causing resistance at the back, but once again, she was interrupted by someone arriving at her front door.

Denny kissed her on the cheek. "Welcome home." He extended a bouquet of yellow roses. "Lovely flowers for the lovely lady."

She thought the roses trembled a bit. *Was he nervous? The great Denny Garter?* "Oh Denny they *are* lovely. Come in for a minute, please. I'll put them in water." As he followed her through to the kitchen, she wondered if she'd dressed appropriately. He looked dashing all in black, but she was comforted that he was actually only wearing jeans and so was she. She wondered how she had forgotten his piercing, dark blue eyes.

"How are your ravioli?"

"Just as I remember. So good, so good. Thank you for bringing me here, Denny. It has always been my favorite place."

"Just as I remember," he echoed her words and grinned.

"Isn't it strange how sometimes we're so close to something great, but rarely take advantage of it? People come from all over to eat these ravioli and even when I lived here, I hardly ever came here. When I was in San Jose for a few months, I was practically next door to the Winchester Mystery House, but never once went there. When I lived in the East Bay, I was at the foot of Mt. Diablo, but never troubled to go to the top of the mountain as tourists do."

"Maybe it's time for a change."

"Apparently."

"It sucks when change is forced on us, right? I was sorry to hear about you and Chuck, really. I'm glad you're back, and I'm really glad you said you'd come out to dinner with me, but I'm sorry."

She shivered at the reminder of rejection and her greatest failure. "Thanks."

"You cold?"

She scoffed. "No, just feeling discarded. Hey, we haven't talked in years. I'm sorry about Wanda too. How are you and Tyler doing?"

"We could use some help." He paused to let her consider what he had said. "Don't get me wrong, he's not a bad kid, but I can't seem to motivate him to do anything. This summer he's been sitting around most of the time playing video games. When I ask him to do something, he says he'll do it, but I think he forgets—that's giving him the benefit of the doubt." Denny chuckled. "He's skinny. Hardly eats anything."

"Who does the cooking?"

"Oh I get by with the basics, like bacon and eggs and sandwiches, but I mostly bring dinners home from the saloon. You should come to our new and improved snack bar. The cook I hired a few years ago added some home cooked choices to the menu. It no longer offers just burgers, hotdogs, and stuff. She does a fried chicken special on Tuesdays, fish and chips on Fridays. Meat loaf on Saturday. She also makes great beans. She's Portuguese. She calls them 'Portuguese Beans.' I think a lot of our regulars *are* regulars because of those beans. Tyler won't touch the beans or anything else that resembles a vegetable." He looked down at his hands, then up to her in a sorrowful, searching way. "The worst part about Tyler is his attitude. He's sullen most of time and pretty much borders on disrespectful. Then I get fed up with it and yell at him. I know I shouldn't. I always feel bad after."

"Then what?" Sherre smiled kindly. "Do you buy him another video game to make up for it?"

Denny raised one eyebrow and his face stuck in a half grin. "You're good. Yeah, it's kinda like that. It's frustrating. I think I try too hard to make up for him not having a mom. Maybe he feels entitled?"

Sherre thought about the old adage, *the apple doesn't fall far from the tree.* "It's possible. I'm certainly no authority on parenting, but it seems like your problems are not unusual. So how are your folks?"

"They're having the time of their lives. Their retirement community is only about an hour and a half north of here. They golf or play tennis every day that it's not too cold or rainy. They have an indoor swimming pool and a lot of friends. They're so busy, I hardly hear from them. They still manage to spoil Tyler though."

Sherre nodded. "Tell them I said, 'hi' next time you see them."

"I will. Thanks. So Sherre, what are your plans for Granzella? Can we talk about that now?" He lifted his eyebrows a bit, his smile was even and smug. "I made an offer to your mom, but I'm willing to make other offers to you."

They launched into a lengthy conversation where Denny was either candid or he was skillful at mentally correcting himself so he sounded candid. Sherre thought he might be telling her what she wanted her to hear. In spite of guarded feelings toward his enthusiasm to help them, she enjoyed him and their lively exchanges. She let herself fall under the spell of his wit, his animal magnetism, and those dark blue eyes, bordered with thick, dark lashes. He was cunning in business, but she sensed sincere concern for the Granzella family. Sherre recognized sincerity when she saw it and considered that he could have tried to take over Granzella Ranch without being so kind. The trials of the past five years seemed to have humbled him. It was gratifying and energizing to hang out with him. She enjoyed his company and felt nurtured as he flirted with her. He made it obvious that he was fascinated with everything she had to say. She felt attractive.

At her door, Denny once again kissed her on the cheek, and then turned to climb up into his truck. After she thanked him for the lovely evening, she stepped inside, and closed the door.

Her heart jumped within her chest when a deep voice within her living room said,

"So you're dating Denny Garter?"

CHAPTER ELEVEN

Seduction

"Chuck! What are you doing here?" She slapped at the wall behind her, and then pushed the top button of the old-fashioned light switch.

"I miss you."

Her voice sounded soft and squeaky. "Obviously, I need to start locking my doors! Um, er I didn't see your truck." Then she said more snidely, "Did Victoria drop you off?"

He chuckled. "No. I parked up at the other end by the cellar." He rose and came close. Towering above her from his six foot three height, he took her purse out of her hand and set it on top of the laptop on her grandfather's desk. Then he took her gently by the shoulders. "You miss me too, right?"

She began shaking. She was angry at herself for being unable to control her body. "How should I answer that, Chuck? Do I miss the life we were building before you slept with someone else?" Her heart held onto a sliver of hope, but she knew hope, when it came to Chuck, could turn out to be a one-way ticket to despair. She felt sad about Chuck, but feeling sad about Chuck was so familiar it was becoming a dangerous habit. Trying to talk herself out of a broken heart, she had courageously declared that she loved enough to lose; felt enough to weep. Her mind continually vacillated between moving on resolutely, shaking off the deteriorated dust their marriage had become, or turning around to fight; take a stand to reclaim her marriage; fix it. And now he was looking penitent.

The apologetic words slipped seductively off of his tongue, warm and honeyed. She began to believe them. "I needed to see you. I'm sorry, Sherre." With a slump to his shoulders he mumbled, "It's over. She broke up with me." He hung his head as if in shame.

Sherre digested this for a few minutes, considering his contrite posture and her own bewilderment. The faint reverberating tone of love refused to die in her heart, some kind of longing that had been answered once, but was now scarred by loss and rejection. Isn't this what she'd prayed for? Didn't she want a chance to repair her marriage? Did she still love him or, did she merely desire not to fail? She knew no marriage was perfect; life wasn't perfect. But she wanted it to be. She heard defeat in her tone when she asked him, "So now what?"

"I was a fool. It's over with Victoria. I want you back." He took one hand off her shoulder and used it to lift her chin. He looked intently into her eyes. "You're the best thing that's ever happened to me." He pleaded in a near whisper, "Will you come back to me? I'll go to counseling. I'll do anything to win you back. Just tell me. What'll it take? I love you, Sherre."

She'd heard him say those exact words at least a million times in her head. She felt vindicated, but Sherre was still struggling, trying to convince herself she was not a fool.

Could she believe him? He'd always been so charming and she had always fallen for his charms. Was Victoria the only one, besides her, who had also fallen for them, or were there others? Could she trust him? Would she, could she, forgive him? She felt the familiar warmth of his body and sensed the fresh, clean scent of Polo Red aftershave that she'd given him for Christmas. "What went wrong, Chuck?"

She saw him flinch at the question. "You were too controlling."

"That's brutally honest. Yet you want to come back now? Aren't you afraid I'll try to control you again?"

"It's worth the risk." He guiltily grinned. "I actually kind of like it when you control me."

"So it wasn't the sex?"

"No," he smiled smugly, as if he knew something she didn't, "in fact how about we—?"

"It's going to take a lot more than that charming smile of yours to seduce me."

"How about my charming touch? He touched the bare skin of her arm "We're still married." When she didn't resist, he put his hand at the base of her back and pushed her body forcefully against his.

She was breathing heavily, "We should talk first. I need to talk about—"

"We'll talk in the morning." He kissed her mouth and lifted her off her feet, and then carried her to the bedroom.

Awakening interrupted a dream where she was trying to understand words that were whispered. She sprang from the bed when the reverberation of a diesel engine roared to life. She reached the front window in time to see Chuck's truck taking the corner at Tom and Deidre's. Her heart felt like it would pound its way out of her chest. She was angry; felt duped. Dizziness caused her to turn around to grab the top of her grandfather's desk. Feeling that her abdomen would explode, she took a deep breath and ran to the bathroom, grabbing the wastebasket en route.

Now there'd be no convincing herself that she was not a fool—her phone rang interrupting the diatribe of self-criticism upon which she was about to embark. She wondered who it could be, but needed to let it go to voice mail.

After she'd composed herself and splashed cold water on her face, she called her sister back. "Hey Deedee."

"Why? Why was Chuck at your house so early this morning?"

Sherre heard her own voice, sounding as if it came from a deep well, which she knew was a deep well of humiliation. "He spent the night. Convinced me last night that it was over with Victoria and that he wanted me back."

"Oh." There was a long pause. "But you talked it over this morning and he had to leave early?"

"Um, that would be no. He left while I was still asleep. I think I heard him whispering to her in my pre-wake up dream."

"Oh Sherre. I'm so sorry. I'll be right there. I just made a pot of coffee. I'll bring it."

CHAPTER TWELVE

Tom

Sherre had beat him to the millroom. Tom had gotten up late so he was grateful to smell the coffee, but sorry he hadn't already had some. He felt horrible; hungover. The morning light burned his brain like wild fire. She would know as soon as she took one look at him that he'd had a rough night. He was hoping Kate would be there also so he wouldn't have to face Sherre one on one.

He wasn't ready to talk to Sherre. He knew she would try to jump in with a step-by-step program on how to fix his life. That's what she did in her self-confident, sometimes condescending way. It worked for her in the merciless corporate world, but he wasn't the only family member who sometimes found her scary. Maybe her bossiness was why her husband found someone else. *Yeah Tom. Blame her. That'll work. What's wrong with me?* Sherre had always been good to him. She was family. Another ugly habit rearing its ugly head. *Who else can I blame instead of accepting responsibility? I know. I'll blame Rob.* Every time Rob pulled a cold beer out of the millroom refrigerator, he'd say, "I wish we could have a beer together." In those days, when Tom was strong, not the crumbling weakling as he was now, he'd quip, "We can, only you'll be the one having it." They would laugh as Tom vicariously enjoyed the cool liquid sliding down Rob's throat.

But in those days, Tom felt abstinence was worth it. He had refused to allow his demons to win. He could not take a chance of losing everything that was important to him. Now he was losing anyway so what was the point? He willingly allowed his habit to return. It helped him slip into forgetfulness, where he had no past, no future, where he existed purely in the moment. Drunk, where his entire body emotionally folded into itself where he envisioned himself smaller and smaller and smaller. He wanted to disappear.

Sherre lifted the coffee pot from the counter. "Good morning. Want coffee?"

"That would be good, yeah."

Sherre handed him a mug and settled herself against the counter. "How are you?"

Tom took a sip and nodded. "Oh you know."

"Do I? How would I know?"

"Well, you know we're in trouble and this is my job. And, you know I miss your dad. He wasn't just a business partner, he was my best friend. In fact, he was my only friend."

"What about Deidre?"

"Yeah. Good Question. What about Deidre?" An ache filled his head. He laughed, a false, hard sound, and then leaned back against the countertop, strategically positioning himself at her side, where she couldn't look him in the eyes. A shaft of sunlight had come through open bay doors bouncing off the shimmering cleanliness of the millroom's cement floor. It slanted across their feet like a spotlight.

Sherre looked down at their bright, warm feet, "So I take it things are not good?"

She was relentless. Tom knew it was her strong point, her ability to fall feet first into someone else's world. "I thought you and Deidre talked about everything."

"She's been silent about any troubles you've had. Maybe it's because I've had troubles of my own."

"Or maybe she's embarrassed to tell you about her behavior."

Sherre jerked her head toward him, "*Her* behavior? Not yours?"

"I'm not proud of my behavior. Yeah, I know I'm drinking too much, but I didn't start until she shut me out. You're not the only one whose spouse has been unfaithful."

Sherre's face went blank, as if she couldn't find the expression that belonged there. "Oh no."

"Oh yeah. Ask her."

"Are you sure?"

He tried to put on a solid look which was silly because it didn't help. It didn't help his headache or his heartache. He felt embarrassment rise to heat his neck. It caused his head to ache even more. "I saw a text message flash across the screen of her phone while she was in the shower. It's password protected so I couldn't get back to it to see who it was from, but I read enough to see it was a love note."

"And, instead of confronting her, you started drinking?"

"Yeah. What's the point? What's left for me? My job? My kids?"

"Well, yes, your kids! And you know I'll do everything I can to save your job. I'm not sure what's going to happen at the Ranch. You may no longer be an owner, but I'll make sure you are compensated and still have work. But Tom, you know you've got to stop, right? Some people can drink a little and it doesn't ruin their lives—"

"Yeah. I know." He hung his head and closed his eyes. "I don't think I can quit, Sherre. I tell myself every morning, I'm done. I can do it, but later in the day, I'm weak. No control. I'm a loser."

"No Tom. You're not a loser. You're a great dad and you've been a great husband to Deidre all these years. You're a great business partner and a hard worker. If you need it, we'll get you help. If I can arrange it, will you go to rehab?"

"Maybe, if I need to, maybe I can try again without it. It's so expensive and there's the harvest—"

"I know, bad timing, but are you willing to go if that's what it'll take?"

"Yeah, if I have to, I'll go. I want to overcome at least one demon."

"Oh honey. I'm so sorry." She slid closer and wrapped her arm around him for a sideways hug. "I'll talk to her. I can hardly believe this."

"Me neither." He intently studied the laces of their tennis shoes and how the bright light also caused dark shadows on the floor. He still felt defeated by his cowardice to retreat into the drink, but it was good to finally tell someone. He told Sherre she wasn't the only one with a cheating spouse. The road ran both ways.

Neither was he the only one. Somehow she was bravely coping and carrying on with life. He could try to conquer this. This family was his family too, not just Deidre's. He had a strong bond of love with his mother-in-law and this incredibly strong sister standing next to him, from whom he could draw strength. A single tear escaped his eye.

CHAPTER THIRTEEN

Sunday Dinner

Francesca, Sherre, Tom, Deidre, Courtney, Tommy, Kate

Sherre busied herself with placemats, silverware, and their best china. This first Sunday dinner since the accident was going to be cathartic for all of them. She was convinced this would help them heal. They needed to bring their separate stages of progress to heal together from the loss of Dad. If what Tom said was true, maybe Deidre would get a reality check; be reminded of Granzella traditions. Family first and Tom was part of it. She realized as she pondered these things, that when she married Chuck, she didn't bring him into the family, but rather left them to start her own life with him. She fought the pain near her heart with a deep breath.

Traditionally, everyone was welcome at their table, even strangers, but Sherre found herself relieved that Darian was absent. He was holding an open house. Their Sunday dinner custom was to prepare abundantly so any family member could invite a guest or guests at the spur of the moment. Sometimes they invited a large family home from church. One time they set a place for a homeless man, who Courtney spotted walking back to Gypsy Clearing from the Burgess Pie Stand.

"Hi Mom, I beat everyone else here." Sherre held her pot-holder hands in the air and kissed her mother on the cheek. "I took out the roast while you were in the back. It's on that platter under the foil. What else do you want me to do?"

"Turn the oven up to 400. It's still hot from the roast so it shouldn't take long. As soon as it gets there, put in the cornbread. Then in ten minutes, put in the veggies. They are dressed with olive oil."

"Of course they are."

"Yes, of course they are."

They said together, "The world's best olive oil," and they giggled.

"The pork roast is so big, I didn't do a lot today. The potatoes are almost ready to mash. Are you okay?"

"I'm kind of not okay." Sherre pressed her lips together. Her lipstick felt gummy. She resisted blurting out the possibility that Deedee was unfaithful to Tom. She needed to talk to Deedee first, and if it was indeed true, it would be up to Deedee to tell her mom, not Sherre. "I don't think I'll be able to fix the problems."

Francesca turned and stared at her daughter for a long moment, and then shook her head as if to physically shake off her thoughts. "Well, it hasn't happened just yet, but you seem to be dreading in advance. This is not like you Sherre. You're wasting energy by suffering twice. Whatever decisions you guide us through, will work out for the best. Maybe—"

"Hi Grandma!" Tommy burst into the kitchen and surrounded Francesca with his arms. "Mom said we could just come in because the Cadillac's not here."

Francesca jerked her head toward Deidre. "Is that true?"

"Yes, Mom. We knock and wait when Darian's here."

Francesca's face turned red. She brought her hands to her face, where everyone noticed the remarkable diamond ring on her left hand.

"Wow! Tommy reached out his right hand and brought Francesca's ring closer. "That's huge."

There was silence as the sisters exchanged glances, and then turned to their mother expecting her to speak, but the doorbell rang.

Sherre said, "I'll get it. That'll be Kate."

Tom helped Francesca place the food on the table, and then he pulled out her chair for her. He stayed on his feet by his chair waiting for the ladies to enter and instructed Tommy to do the same. The rest of his family settled around the table in their usual spots.

After introducing Kate to Deidre and the kids, Sherre took her place, facing the window at an angle. She loved to watch the birds in the hearty trumpet vine. The hummingbirds visited regularly, but presently a flock of sparrows were twittering maniacally and hopping from the lower branches to the ground and then back up. "Kate, please sit here next to me." She patted the seat next to her that shared the same view.

Kate said, "I can't believe how great it smells in here!"

"Yeah Mom has a knack for it. She cooks a pork roast for hours with a lot of garlic and, of course, olive oil, and when she roasts vegetables, she includes leeks. I'm surprised you didn't smell it down at your temporary home."

"Actually, I smelled it long before I got close. Yum!"

Francesca asked a blessing on the food, thanked God that Kate had joined them, and then asked God to bless Kate.

When Kate lifted her chin, Sherre noticed unshed tears.

"So Kate. Welcome to our Italian family dinner. I know it's actually lunch, but on Sunday, when we do this after church, we call it dinner. And, following in the tradition of our Italian roots, we really, really try not to talk business. But, of course, it sometimes creeps up to the table because our business is so much a part of our lives. We do get kind of personal though, so I apologize in advance if it seems a bit personal for you. In fact, I was about to do just that. When you rang the doorbell, we had all just noticed that two or three karat rock on my mom's left hand. So you'll get the full story first hand, first told." Sherre thought she saw disappointment bleed into Kate's expression, but decided that it could not be possible, having only met Francesca and Darian once before. "So Mom, full disclosure. Had to be last night, right?"

Francesca cleared her throat self-consciously. Her voice sounded husky as she began, "Yes. He asked me to dress for fine dining. He took me all the way to a country club in Stockton that he belongs to. He called ahead and requested that the chef prepare Veal Osso Buco. He ordered a bottle of Dom Perignon Champagne. Got down on one knee, the whole romantic tradition. He said he knew he couldn't ask my father, but if I wanted to wait to answer until he could ask you," she looked to her right at Deidre, and then across the table at Sherre, "he would be patient for an answer."

"Really?" Shock coursed through Sherre but she tried hard to mask it. "He would really risk asking our permission? That was a bold move." She tried to picture the romantic scene and tried to draw herself into romantic feelings for her mother's sake, but the image was vague and movie-ish, more to her like a scary thriller than a love story.

Francesca faced Kate directly. "My family, as you can probably tell, is less than over-joyed—"

"Oh Mom," Deidre interrupted, "we're just shocked. Please give us a chance—"

It was Francesca's turn to interrupt, "You see Kate, my husband, their father," she waved her hand between Sherre and Deidre, "only died nine months ago."

Kate said. "Yes. I know. Sherre mentioned it. I'm sorry for your loss, but happy for your new hope."

Sherre had only known Kate for a few days, but found herself once again interpreting Kate's response, thinking Kate was being polite, rather than happy about the engagement.

Francesca said grimly, "Thank you! I'm glad someone is happy." She talked over the emerging grunts of protest from her daughters and continued to direct her conversation toward Kate, using her presence as a buffer. "Memories are a comfort once the pain dies down. I'm not going to forget my first love, the father of my children, and the grandfather of my grandchildren." Her voice strained with emotion and lifted slightly in pitch. "His name was Roberto, but we called him Rob." She lifted her chin and straightened her already upright back. The water that had gathered in her eyes subsided when she took a deep breath. "Loneliness is like a knife in the chest. In some ways, I'd been lonely for a long time. The girls know this. I loved their father and he loved me, but he wasn't all that emotionally available to any of us. He would *do* anything physical or material for us, but emotional intimacy was not his forté." She looked down at the giant diamond on her finger. "Not long after Rob died, I met Darian. I think he understands that the love in our future cannot, and will not, eliminate my love in the past."

Everything about her mother seemed clenched. Sherre felt horrible and responsible. How could she and Deidre be honest without sucking the joy from a moment like this? She got up from the table and came around to hug her mom. "I love you Mom and I'm happy you're happy."

Deidre's arms wrapped around both of them. "Me too."

All three apologized for tears. Deidre grabbed a few tissues from the box on the kitchen counter. There were deep giggles as they mopped up.

"So" Sherre said, "What else do we have to talk about today?"

Kate piped up, "Well, I'd like to say that I'm honored to be sitting at this table with your candid, devoted family. And this food is delicious! Seriously, so delicious. This meat is so tender and juicy. It tastes even better than it smelled."

Courtney had been staring into space as though she could see something which was invisible to the rest of them. Her face was gentle and beautiful, touched with a kind of wonder. As if it were perfect timing for her to take up the baton and offer something else they should talk about today, she asked, "Aunt Sherre. How was your dinner with Mr. Garter?" She sat calm and erect.

Sherre felt the answer was too big to get out in words. "Um. Well, for starters, it was much more enjoyable than I expected it to be." She wasn't ready to confess to her family that she was thinking about his proposals. Think! All she could do was think. As if she were thinking with more than one brain. A tangle of competing thoughts collided often passing too quickly to hold. Thoughts about Chuck. Thoughts about Denny. Thoughts about their dire financial straits. "He seems to have mellowed over the past five years."

Deidre scoffed. "I wouldn't count on it."

Sherre turned to Kate, "Denny Garter's the neighbor whose property runs along our entire western property line."

Kate grinned, "The one whose varmints we needed to bait?"

"Yes. He's been known to let parts of his ranch go. To be fair though, he's got a lot of land, a lot of responsibility, and several other businesses."

"Like the Garter Saloon that I passed on my way here?"

"Yes. Boy, you don't miss a thing! That, plus he owns the strip mall surrounding the saloon and another down by Jackson that includes the busiest gas station in the county."

Deidre's tone was accusatory, "Don't make excuses for him Sherre. You didn't fall for his charms did you?"

Sherre felt her neck go red. "I'm just saying he was nice. We were friends in high school, you know. He, oh I don't know, he was cool and smooth. He didn't try to railroad me into anything if that's what you're asking." She was certain her neck was approaching the color of a beet. Changing the subject a bit she asked, "Courtney, how did you know I went to dinner with him?" She looked at her mother. "Grandma was the only one that knew."

Francesca shook her head.

"Tyler told me."

Tommy braced his arms on the table and leaned in toward Courtney. "You la-la-love him don't you, don't you, don't you?"

"No."

"Seriously?"

"I'm only ever serious, don't you know? I only want to find adequate opportunity to help him." Courtney turned to Kate, "His mother left them, Miss Stryker."

"Oh sweetheart, please call me Kate. You too, Tommy." She turned to Deidre and Tom. "Gosh. You are sure doing a great job of teaching these delightful children manners. Courtney, you were saying you wanted to help him and that his mother abandoned him?"

Sherre could tell that Courtney liked Kate. Sherre rarely got to see that sweet smile that was on Courtney's face, including in the corners of her eyes, as she continued, "Mrs. Garter is Tyler's mother, but he was born before she married Mr. Garter. Mr. Garter adopted Tyler, then Mrs. Garter left."

Here in the daylight, detached from Denny's smooth words, his handsome looks, and his confident promises, Sherre found that she still felt sympathetic toward him. She looked at Deedee and said, "I think all that he's been through has changed him from the young man we knew in high school, so full of pride and self-assurance into a better man with less regard for himself."

Tom said, "Yes. I've noticed a change in him since he took on the role of single dad. And it humbles a man when his wife cheats on him." He carefully examined the roasted Brussels sprouts on his plate.

Sherre looked at Deidre, who had frozen mid-chew and had turned to face Tom. Her face had lost all expression and all color had drained from it. The only sounds in the room were from silverware touching a plate or water glasses being set on the table, and the soft, too intimate sounds of chewing.

Tommy broke the silence with, "You love Tyler, you la-la-love him."

"Tommy that's enough," Tom shot an authoritative frown in his direction.

His sister retorted, "Yes. Stop it. I don't like it. Haven't you got someone else to annoy?"

"Sure, lots a people, but you're so perfect and you're my sister."

Chapter Fourteen

Deidre

"So, Deedee, how're you doing?" Sherre was seated at Deidre's kitchen table. Holding the handle of her tea mug, her wrist felt a little sticky as she rested it on the table. She was trying to disregard the smell of the dishes piled in the sink, the overflowing garbage canister, and the grime on the linoleum floor that was particularly thick near the baseboards and the corners.

"Pretty good." Her tone was guarded.

The silence between them swelled and filled the room; a fly buzzed angrily against the kitchen window screen. Sherre knew that technique. She'd used it a million times in the past four out of five years of her marriage. However in that venue, Sherre was reasonably sure that Chuck did not really want to know how Sherre was. He willingly accepted her guarded replies of, "fine," most likely with relief. But, Sherre truly desired to know how her sister was. She wanted to fix Deedee's problems for Deedee's sake of course, but also, if she could admit it to herself, to bolster her own ego. Sherre's world, and her control of it, were unraveling. First her marriage, then the Ranch's troubles, then her mother's dubious engagement, and now, if her brother-in-law's suspicions were correct, her sister was having an affair. "I don't believe you. You don't even sound like you've convinced yourself that things are pretty good."

Deidre sat down across from Sherre with her own mug of tea. "Ew! This table is gooey. Sorry. Tommy must have gotten carried away with the syrup bottle on his toaster waffle this morning." She sighed and looked around her kitchen. "I wish you would have given me more of a heads-up. I've been really busy lately. Haven't been keepin' things up like I usually do."

"It's perfectly fine. I didn't come to see your house. I came to see you." Sherre smiled and didn't challenge Deedee's proclamation that she "usually did." In fact, she usually didn't. Sherre's comfortable arrival at Grandpa Bob's was a testimony to Deidre's ability to clean and organize, but throughout Deidre's life, she hadn't really given cleaning priority, unless company was coming. "Why are you so busy in the summer? I'm not a mom, but I would've thought things would calm down in the summer."

"Oh they do, but they're ramping up again. I took the kids clear to Stockton yesterday for some back to school shopping. And," Sherre deduced a splash of pink rising in Deidre's neck and cheeks, "I've been helping out at the school. You know. Getting the classrooms ready. I was Tommy's homeroom mom last year and Mr. Taylor asked me to create a file to organize things for the next homeroom volunteer. He really appreciated the way I did things." Her neck was now fully red.

"Is Tom right? Are you having an affair?"

Deidre had a surprised look on her face, but she answered calmly, without defensiveness. Sherre thought maybe Deidre felt relieved,

"Um, not exactly. I wondered yesterday when Tom said that at dinner … Tom knows?"

"By any chance, is Mr. Taylor the person with whom you're 'um, not exactly' having an affair?"

Deidre bowed her chin to her chest. She whispered, "I'm so ashamed. We didn't mean for it to happen."

"I'm sure no one ever does."

Deidre looked at Sherre pleadingly, "Please believe me. We haven't done anything except talk."

"Is he married too?"

"No. I wouldn't—oh I can't say that can I? I question myself now about what I wouldn't do. When we said our vows, I never thought I would love anyone else besides Tom. But Tom doesn't understand me. Heck, he doesn't *really* talk to me. Trying to get him to talk about anything vaguely emotional, rather than factual, is like watching an uncoordinated man attempting to look cool on a dance floor. He's incapable. His idea of intimacy is sex without foreplay or afterplay, if that's a word. When I'm with Jeff, we get each other, just by looking at each other. My eyes speak for me. His eyes speak for him. He's so interesting, so kind, so engaged."

"And so busted."

"What do you mean?"

"Tom saw a text come through on your phone while you were in the shower. It was too fast for him to read entirely before the screen went black, but he knew it was a love note."

Deidre's face was colorless now except for dark circles that materialized beneath her eyes, "I'm probably the reason he started drinking again."

"He seems to think so too."

"Yeah, before we got married, he told me he was totally out of control when he was a teenager and it carried on into his twenties. He said meeting me was what helped him admit he had a real problem and it motivated him to get help. I don't know if you knew, but he went to AA meetings for the first few years we were married, but he hasn't gone to any for a very long time."

"I'm not sure you can take all that blame. I've been thinking about us Granzella women, starting with Mom. We seem to settle for dysfunctional men. In fact, so much so that I'm leery about your Jeff's character."

"He's not *my* Jeff!" Then less indignantly, she asked, "Are you saying that Dad was dysfunctional?"

Sherre nodded. "Maybe. I'm afraid, to one degree or another, all of our men have been. Dad, Chuck, Tom, and probably Jeff. And, I'm not sure about Denny, but I'm feeling myself sucked into his orbit—"

"No!" Deidre rose from the table and started pacing in the kitchen and at intervals making unendurable squeaking sounds, while sucking her lower lip beneath her top teeth. Sherre could hear Deedee's tennis shoes pull loose from the syrupy floor with each step.

"For goodness sake, Deedee, please sit down."

She did, and then she said, "Do you think I'm crazy?"

"A little bit at the moment."

"That's helpful."

"I know, but if we can figure out what's causing us to act a little bit crazy, maybe we can alter our course and start behaving in a way that's best for our future, and the future of your children. All this craziness, including Mom's is what triggered my obsession with this analysis of our dysfunction. And Darian is in a whole dysfunctional class of his own. There's something about his eyes that seem so distant. He's so shifty. One moment he's all charming and seemingly sweet. The next his facial expressions go dark, looking void of feeling. The scariest part is the way he subtly tries to charm you and me, not just overtly charm Mom. I'm wondering about his statement that he would wait for our approval. Do you think he already thinks he's got us hornswoggled?"

Deidre laughed. "Hornswoggled? Where'd you learn that word, Texas?"

Sherre giggled too. "Probably. I dunno. But, seriously. I felt terrible yesterday when Mom told us how Darian was so romantic—"

"Yeah me too, but he's like a, I'm not sure what he's like. He seems evil."

"He reminds me of the slick serpent that Satan indwelled to tempt Eve in the Garden of

Eden." She shivered. "Am I overthinking this, or overreacting?"

"Gosh. I don't know. Mom's no dummy."

"But she may be a bit dysfunctional too, which brings me back to my point. Don't get me wrong. I know Dad was a great guy in so many ways. He was so generous to all of us, including Mom, but his generosity was mostly material, especially to Mom. He seemed to set up emotional barriers. I'm not sure why. He would have done anything for any of us, but did you notice that we usually had to ask? Anything that was volunteered was Mom's idea and from her prompting."

"Hmmm. Yeah. I suppose that's true. I wonder if it goes way back. To Grandpa or even Great-Grandpa."

"I was thinking the same thing. Mom opened up to me a little the other day. It think Darian is sweeping her off her feet so easily because Dad created a vacuum, not just by dying."

Deidre scoffed and then giggled. "I bet you told yourself you weren't going to lecture me about cleaning my house, but here ya go talking about sweeping and vacuums."

Sherre chuckled, "You're so silly. You know one of the things that's great about you, Deedee? You've always put people first. You'd prefer to have your house perfect before letting anyone in through your front door, but you never turn anyone away if it's not. Your heart and home is always open to all. I'm hoping your graciousness and kindness will override the propensity for dysfunction that Tommy will definitely get from his father."

Deidre's eyes glistened. "Thanks for that." She grabbed a napkin from the holder in the center of the table and dabbed her eyes, then her nose. She looked toward the heap on top of the garbage canister as if she would toss the napkin, but changed her mind and wadded it into her fist. "So why do you think we are dysfunctional man fans?"

"I have a theory."

"Pray tell."

"You know that outdoor metal table in front of the coffee shop at Denny's strip mall? The one with one leg shorter than the others?"

"Yeah drives me crazy whenever we get that one."

"What if you and I were sitting at the table, trying to have a cuppa and some conversation and the table kept clunking? Then, what if one of us, let's say it's me, decides to be a hero? I lean on the table with one elbow and hold the darned thing steady for the rest of our stay. When I get up, I'm bent. I go forward with a one shoulder forward, a bent arm, and a crooked spine. And I stay that way because my bent position has become my new normal. My reengineered comfort zone affects my future choices so I make warped choices."

"Why are you so smart?"

"You're silly. I just think a lot. Chuck said I thought too much. Said I overanalyzed everything."

"Well we already know he's a stupid-head. And I'm going to think about your theory. I like it. The sins of the parents visited on the third and fourth generation." Deidre grinned. "So we can blame Mom and, of course, Dad."

Sherre chuckled. "Yeah, I suppose we could, but I think it would be better not to blame, but retrain ourselves and put a stop to it. Straighten up and walk right. Tom's willing to change, Deedee. I talked to him. If you talk to him, work this out, and help him straighten up, maybe this doesn't need to pass to Courtney and Tommy."

Deidre's eyes brimmed again. She snatched another napkin. "You're right. I know you're right. I should quit flirting with Jeff—flirting with danger—and focus on healing my own dysfunction, and concentrate on my husband and my kids." She broke down fully then. After a full mop up, hearty sniff, and a sip of tea, she said, "I'm not sure I can though. I think I'm in love with Jeff."

Sherre reached across the table to pat Deidre's fist that now held three wadded napkins. "I'm certainly not the poster child for saving a marriage, Deedee, and therefore probably not the best counselor, but from here it looks like you might not be in love, just infatuated with someone who is kind and accepting of you. Would you consider talking to a real counselor?"

Deidre looked up with her swollen red eyes. "Yeah. I suppose I could do that." Then she grinned. "Maybe the counselor will tell me I *am* in love with Jeff."

Sherre scoffed. "You wicked woman!"

"I know, I know. I'm kidding. I need to quit flirting with danger, but I'm not sure I can."

"Well at least you're willing to talk to someone about it. I wish I could convince Mom that she's flirting with danger."

CHAPTER FIFTEEN

Another Dinner

*Francesca, Sherre, Tom, Deidre,
Courtney, Tommy, Kate, Darian*

"I could get used to this," Kate said. "I never realized how great it was to work the land; to be a rancher." She didn't add, to be part of a ranching family. "You *made* these ravioli, Francesca?"

Francesca blushed. "Yup. These are my veal ravioli. We seem to like them best with this meat sauce. Some Sunday, before you leave, I'll make my cheese ravioli. I usually put some into this sauce and some into Alfredo."

"I may never leave."

"Works for me," said Sherre. "Hey, Kate and I ran into Grandma Dorothy's cousin, Freddy Burgess at the Farmer's Market on

Wednesday." She felt a fresh wave of grief remembering Grandma Dorothy, even though she'd been gone for a few years ... and then Grandpa Bob died about a year later.

Tom said, "Really? How is Freddy? How're his crops this year?"

"He said it's a bad year for corn. The ears don't seem to completely fill in. He's selling most of it to cattle breeders this year. Oh! You know what else he said? He said they found a body down by the river at Gypsy Clearing and, so far, the Sheriff is considering it a homicide."

"Yikes!" said Deidre. "Do they know who it was?"

"Not yet, Cousin Freddy said they think he may have been a homeless guy."

Courtney looked distressed. "Why would anyone murder a homeless man?"

Sherre noticed an alteration in Darian's demeanor. His attention was unnerving as if he'd become porous, soaking in every detail. She glanced at her mother and thought about how people so often cause a disruption in the lives of those around them by following their hearts.

"Why is it called Gypsy Clearing?" Darian blinked his strangely delicate eye lashes and set down his fork. His movements were jerky. He avoided meeting her eyes.

Sherre thought she saw an expression of brutality fly across his face as fast as the click of the camera. It was there and gone so quickly, she could almost believe she'd imagined it, but she knew she hadn't imagined it because reading faces was one of her skills.

Francesca replied, "In the seventies and eighties, gypsies frequented that clearing by the river, annually, sometimes staying most of the summer. I heard that they would move on to Arizona when the weather turned cold here. They haven't been back since—" She paused.

"It's okay, Mom. I don't think Lois or Johnny would mind you telling their story." Deidre smiled at Courtney and Tommy.

Tommy said, "There's a story about the gypsies? Cool. I saved a story for dinner too. We found two mice in Cassie's water pan this morning. I think one fell in trying to get a drink and yelled," Tommy's pitch went high and squeaky, "Help! Help! And the other mouse jumped in to save her." He started giggling and lost control.

Sherre was compelled to laugh too, as always, when she heard Tommy's laugh.

Tommy braced his arms on the table and leaned in, "We could laugh our heads off, huh, Aunt Sherre? Ha-ha-ha, thud, thud." He lost control again, and this time Sherre, Deidre, and Tom all broke into giggles and laughter. Courtney smiled as though she were entertained.

Kate smiled as if she were taking in the dynamics of the conversation, how they simply changed subjects, circled back, occasionally contended with each other, yet carried on with family comradery. Then in her chic elfin way, she also erupted in laughter. Iced tea sloshed precariously in her glass.

Darian appeared to be wrestling with an inner fury. "Someone murdered a man a few miles from here." Was it a sick fascination, like someone with road hazard interest?

Sherre noticed that his expression had turned hostile, his eyes were like flint. She wondered how her mother kept up with his moods or how he himself kept up with them.

Tommy calmed himself from laughing and piped up again, "Maybe the man found gold in the river and someone killed him for it." He tore his bread in half, sending a rich cascade of crumbs into his lap.

Tom said, "Son, people are always finding gold in our rivers and streams, but not enough to get murdered for."

Darian put one elegantly buffed nail on top of his fork before lifting it properly, "Gold," was all he said, as if saying it to himself.

Courtney said, "I want to hear the gypsy story. Why don't they come here anymore?"

Kate set down her fork and said, "I'd like to hear it too."

So Francesca related as much as she knew about John's kindness to the gypsy father, Lois' encounter with the pregnant gypsy mother, and how Johnny was left on their porch. "And never again have any gypsy caravans returned to the clearing, but the name of the camp lived timelessly on as names do." She looked at

Sherre, "And I'm sure love lives timelessly on as well."

Sherre replied, "Of course, Lois loves Johnny—"

"Oh Sherre," Deidre scoffed, "You mean you haven't figured out why Johnny is down repairing your house in all his spare time? Do you think he hasn't noticed that Denny's trying to make his move and that Chuck is, well," she looked compassionately at Sherre, "toying with your emotions."

"What?" Francesca looked up from a bite of ravioli, "Chuck?"

From across the table, Sherre could feel her mother flinch.

"Yeah," Deidre said, "he came over the other night, begged her to come back to him, and said it was over with the trollop."

Sherre felt the heat on her neck and her cheeks. "But it's not over between them. He was, I'm sure, as Deedee said, just toying with me."

Tom and Deidre looked steadily at each other and then turned away, as if there were new rules of life that they had yet to settle.

Tommy asked the question, "What's a trollop?"

Courtney said, "A vulgar or disreputable
woman; especially one who engages in sexual
promiscuity."

Deidre smiled at her daughter and asked,
"Did you look it up?"

"That is correct. Tyler said he overheard
heard Denny use that label for his mother so I
looked it up on my phone. Then Tyler said, in
a very strange voice, 'That is correct. I looked it
up too.'" Her nostrils twitched and her eyes
thought off to the side. "He may have been
mimicking me." She muttered something
under her breath, "I am accustomed to inad-
vertently creating amusement."

"Oh honey," said Deidre, "Yes, he probably
was mimicking you, but I don't think he
wanted to laugh at you. I think it was because
he really likes you."

"Yeah, he la-la-loves you."

Tom said, "Enough!" He glowered across
the table at his son.

Amusement etched Darian's deceptively
easygoing voice, "So Sherre, did I hear all this

correctly, no offense, Courtney," he narrowed his eyes to a slit and gave Courtney a snide grin, and then turned back to Sherre, "your ex wants you back, the Calaveras land baron is trying to court you, and the adopted gypsy has always been in love with you?"

Sherre had a mean feeling in her chest like heartburn. There was an unquiet chatter in her mind since her mother and sister stated so emphatically that Johnny had always been in love with her. Could that be true? Was she so blind that she didn't know the difference between a lifelong friend and someone who was in love with her? She had certainly proved, without a doubt, that she was blind regarding Chuck! She'd behaved like a fool and could no longer justify her foolishness under the guise of forgiveness or the worthy intention to save a sinking marriage. It was a struggle to settle her mind on a coherent thought. It needed to take time out to analyze her years of friendship with Johnny. The only thing she knew for sure was that she resented Darian's flippant, insensitive remark directed at Courtney when he over-emphasized the word "correctly." Sherre's assessment of Darian Danville was that he was mean, or even, as someone once sang, "bad to the bone." She gave Darian an over-polished smile. "Sounds about right."

CHAPTER SIXTEEN

Francesca

There were so many nights over the past nine months when the ache of her loss became as familiar as breathing; Francesca had trouble falling asleep. When she finally slept, waves of terror often woke her to a damp nightgown. A video in her head repeatedly replayed the phone call that interrupted her when she was about to pour boiling water out of the tea kettle into the tea pot. Her husband's truck was T-boned by car driven by an older woman, who turned out to be Darian's grandmother.

She met Darian at the funeral. The first time she looked into his gray eyes, she found something her aching heart hadn't expected to find. She thought she saw a deep compassion for her. He seemed to know how to comfort her, and then before she realized what was happening, he professed that their friendship was so much more to him. He convinced her he was unable to resist her beauty, kindness, and wisdom, and that he had fallen deeply in love with her.

Now insomnia was imposing new, altered pictures onto the video screen of Francesca's nightmares. A phone call notified her that this time she had lost Darian. The first time that scene played, Darian had had an accident similar to Rob's. Last week, she woke in soaking sweat, having watched Darian fall to his death off the edge of a tall water tower. It seemed so real, she kept trying to work it out, in spite of her awareness that she was dreaming. Why he was up there in the first place? She pondered if she was already reciprocating Darian's professed love.

Tonight's video played after she'd drifted into deep sleep. He had been showing a house and, just like that house in Florida that was on the news, a sinkhole swallowed the room he was in. They never found his body.

"Hello, Beautiful." Darian pulled her toward him and caressed her back. "Are we alone?"

He smelled like shampoo, sunscreen, and sensuous aftershave. "Yes, but Darian, I'm not going to bed with you. Quit asking." Francesca was tempted. Even to her own ears, her rejection sounded more playful than insistent.

"Not until we're married?"

"Yes. I told you. That's my standard."

"Then let's get married."

She gave a jerk of her chin. A block of sun poked through the morning clouds, warmed her shoulder, and splayed across the gleaming kitchen countertop, but she felt a sharp chill. "You mean set a date and start making arrangements?"

"No. I mean now. Today. Let's skip all that," He grinned in a way that Francesca thought was almost malicious. "I feel it here, my darling." His hand gestured towards his breast. "I'm attracted to you, yes, and how! But this is love. Let's make it permanent."

"But, we don't have a marriage license we need a blood —"

He interrupted her. "We don't need a blood test anymore, not even in California. I checked, but if we go to Reno, the marriage license bureau is open every day until midnight." He stroked the outside of her arm. "And there are nice wedding chapels everywhere, just waiting for us to pick one. It's only two hours away."

"Um, wow! You've really thought this through. But, what about my daughters, and Tom, and the kids?"

He narrowed his eyes, and one side of his mouth went up, "Do you really think they want to be at our wedding? If so, we can invite them to come with us."

Francesca felt her heart accelerate to its familiar staccato when she was in the powerful orbit of Darian's smooth words, handsome looks and confident promises. She recalled her recent dreams. Were they a message from God reminding her that life is short? *Would Deidre and Sherre want to come? Maybe so, but probably not.* Sherre asked her not to rush into anything, but if she didn't marry Darian soon, she knew she'd take him into her bed and she definitely didn't want that. *I'm an old fashioned woman,* she giggled, *like Elizabeth Taylor. How many times was Liz married anyway?*

The sun slid behind a cloud, causing the room to suddenly become comparatively dark.

"Why'd you giggle?"

She felt a tentative smile lift the lower half of her face. "Let's do it."

He nodded with approval and stepped back to look at her. He clasped his thin, beautiful hands together so they made a pointed church roof, and then he broke the imaginary church apart and fluttered one set of fingers toward the back of the house and Francesca's bedroom. "Pack a bag. We'll stay at the finest hotel we can find in Reno tonight."

Francesca nodded seriously but didn't say anything.

Darian waited, his domineering silence maintaining command.

Finally, as if she'd found a solid reason to change her mind, she said, "But the chickens—"

He furrowed his brows, but maintained a smug grin. "I'll put 'em away early—right now, while you're packing your bag." His fixed expression of victory was starting to make his face twitch. "You've got a first-class set up for them with those tubes for feed and clean water. They'll be okay if you're gone for one day, right?"

"Um, maybe, but please turn on the misters. I don't want them to get hot by being cooped up all day. I'll ask Johnny to turn off the water at sunset and give them some treats. He probably won't mind." She giggled again. "I can't believe we're doing this."

He took her in his arms again and kissed her passionately. Then breathing softly into her ear, "Believe it. You know it's going to happen anyway. Let's start our happy-ever-after today." He stroked her in a forbidden way.

"Darian, really, I want to wait." She stepped back, held up her hand, and swallowed vigorously, the tendons of her throat springing out. "I'll go pack. I'll text Johnny on the way. What about you? We'll need to stop at your place for an overnight bag, right?" She felt her face hot with color.

"Mine's in the car. I've had one ready for a long time, hoping you'd invite me to spend the night."

CHAPTER SEVENTEEN

New Family Dinner Dynamics

Sherre, Tom, Deidre, Courtney, Tommy, Kate, Mr. & Mrs. Darian Danville

"Mom just texted me. They'll be here in a few minutes." Deidre was setting the table. "I guess we should set Darian at the head now." Sherre thought Deedee looked radiant *I wonder if she's been doing a lot of volunteer work at school.*

Sherre sighed, "Yeah. Let's put him in that spot at the table that used to be Dad's." They had both been in a daze since their mother had called Deedee, who seemed to be coping more competently than Sherre felt. Then, Francesca asked Deidre not to call Sherre until Francesca reached Sherre herself. Sherre's emotions were all over the place, vacillating between anger, confusion, and denial. Her deepest sadness, however, centered on not being invited to the wedding. She felt sorry for her mother, who didn't feel supported enough by her daughters to invite them, and she felt insulted, on behalf of her sister and herself, that they'd moved downward in their mother's affections.

Courtney, Tommy, and Kate spilled in through the dining room door, a tumble of noise and movement and different fragrances as if there were ten of them not just three. "Dad's on his way," said Tommy. We were on our way back from the chicken coup and saw him when he came out of the Black Hole. He said he's going down to the house to clean up."

"Black hole?" asked Kate.

"Yeah, our cell phones don't work in a lot of pockets around here." She smiled. "We've been calling them 'the Black Hole' for so long, I'd forgotten that others would be clueless about what we're talking about. The millroom is one of those pockets. Tom can sometimes get a text there, but not send one. And phone calls are impossible." Sherre said, "So Kate, did you have a nice couple of days away from all of this?"

Kate smiled, "Yes, I did, but I'm glad to be back out in the quietness of the country. I'm loving it out here and I'm acquiring a love for olive oil ranching."

"Even the nasty chores, like counting insects in stinky yeast?" Courtney asked incredulously.

Everyone knowingly giggled or chuckled, as each remembered their own encounters with putrid fruit flies.

"Yeah, in spite of that most unpleasant task, I could get used to living in this world."

The wheeze of the screen door stopped all conversation. Sherre felt a knot in her stomach.

"They're here," said Courtney.

"Or it's Dad," said Tommy.

Darian gallantly disconnected Francesca's arm that was looped through his and held her hand above her head, leading her ahead of him through the door to the kitchen. Then following behind her he bowed, rose and said, "Ladies and gentlemen, may I present Mrs. Francesca Danville?"

Sherry had to admit that his presentation was a welcome, ice breaking gesture. Everyone, even Courtney, enthusiastically applauded.

Sherre heard a contrived patronizing tone to Deedee's voice and knew her own sounded slightly Pollyanna, but they got through the congratulations the best they could.

The only way they knew Francesca was laughing was by the way in which her shoulders shook. "I know it's crazy for me to worry, but does anyone know how my chickens are?"

Did Sherre see Darian's face twist with distaste of some sort, possibly envy? She was surprised how sullen he seemed. Not the way she remembered Chuck as a newlywed. *Self! That is not allowed. I'm not going to think about Chuck.*

Tommy piped up. "I helped Johnny let them out this morning and we gave them treats. Kate, Courtney and I were just down there visiting them."

Francesca wrapped her arm around her grandson. "Thank you, sweetheart."

Kate seemed to feel at home, "This Mexican food looks delicious. Did you make everything from scratch, even these tortilla chips?"

Deidre said, "Well, we didn't make the tortillas from scratch, but yeah, we cut tortillas up and fried them to make chips. And we made the beans from scratch. Wait till you taste the beans and rice. We're sort of famous for them."

"Why's that?"

Deidre, Sherre, and Francesca all replied together, "It's the olive oil."

When Tom came in, all but Sherre had settled at the table. He kissed his sister-in-law's cheek and said, "A kiss for the cook. Looks and smells great, sister."

Sherre eyes narrowed. She and Tom exchanged knowing glances. His breath smelled strongly of beer. "Thanks. Deedee and I have been cooking most of the day."

Tom waited for Sherre to take her spot at the table, and then sat down and crossed his arms. He grinned at Deidre like she was telling a particularly excellent joke. "Good job, wife. Thanks." He kept smiling but there was no longer any conviction there.

Deidre looked flustered by his omission to kiss the other cook as well as his sarcastic tone. She said somewhat sarcastically, "You're welcome."

Within the awkward silence, everyone was staring at Tom. "Oh!" He got up from his chair and stumbled a little on his way to Francesca's chair. He kissed her on the cheek and said, "Congratulations, Mom." He stuck his hand out to Darian. "And to you. One of the luckiest men on earth."

Darian shook Tom's hand, but the awkwardness persisted.

Kate rescued the conversation with, "Tom. Please sit back down. We've been waiting for you. Not only am I starving but this all looks so good, I'm going to start drooling if we don't ask a blessing soon."

With great deliberation, Tom kept his balance, and then sat down. "Okay." He paused to cover his mouth for a slight burp, and then continued, slurring his words slightly, "Who's gonna pray on this momentous furrst din-ner with Mr. and Mrs. Danville?"

Sherre wasn't ready to talk to God about the marriage just yet, especially in front of the rest of the family, but she could no longer endure the dreadfully uncomfortable silence. She opened her mouth, but Courtney spoke first, "I'll pray. Thank you God for this food. Thank you that Grandma Francesca is married again. Please bless this food to the nourishment of our bodies."

Kate's shoulders were vibrating slightly. When she lifted her head, she was smiling at Sherre as if to communicate, *she's so darned cute.* "So Sherre, you said you had another date with Denny coming up?"

"Yeah. He's taking me to the State Fair."

Tommy said, "State Fair? Can *we* go Dad?"

"Yeah. You're going to help me in the olive oil booth, remember?

"Aw. I want to go on the rides and pan for gold!"

"No gold panning at the State Fair."

Kate giggled, "A date with Denny at the fair should be fun. Fried food and carnival rides always provides opportunity to impress a date with intestinal extravaganzas."

Sherre giggled too. "Right? It's okay. Denny and I have been friends for a lot of years. I don't need to impress him. In fact, I'm not sure we'll ever be anything except just good friends."

"No fire?" This from Darian, who held his profile serenely, like someone accustomed to being admired from all angles. "I'm sorry," he said, not sounding the tiniest bit sorry.

"Not really. It's more like, well, just comfortable." She felt uncomfortable with his questions and wondered why she resented Darian so much. "But you know what? Right now, with all this other stuff going on, comfortable is nice."

Kate nodded with her mouth moving after tearing off a bite of taco with her teeth.

"Miss Str—, I mean Kate, would you really like to move out here to the country?"

"I would, Courtney. On the road, on the way here from Stockton, as the towns got smaller and the houses got farther apart, I felt a peacefulness come over me that I've never known in my life. And, besides that, I've never had friends like you. I like you." She grinned.

"Do you like me too?" Asked Tommy.

Most of them chuckled.

"I do like you too, Tommy. I like you all a lot. You have been so kind to me and so accepting. You were so helpful, teaching me how to take care of the chickens, explaining that premier set up your grandma has provided for them, and patiently answering all my dumb questions."

"Dad says, 'There's no such thing as a dumb question,'" Courtney looked toward Tom, who looked like he was going to fall asleep and faceplant into his refried beans. "Right, Dad?"

Tom's head jerked up, "Huh? Oh right. I think I need some water." He sheepishly took a deep drink from the glass in front of him.

"I'll teach you lots of stuff if you stay Kate. We have two steers out in the field past the chicken coup too. Do you want to meet them?"

"Um. I'm not sure. Are you raising them for food?"

"Um hm. The taco meat you are eating is from the one from last year."

Kate giggled. "Then no thank you. I understand the circle of life. When I eat meat, I have great awareness that a life was sacrificed that I might live, but if you are going to eat 'em I don't want to meet 'em."

Tommy looked at her carefully, seeming to ponder her words, and then he nodded. "Yeah. I get that. Thanks. I never thought about it that way. Something was sacrificed that I might live."

"If I do stay in the valley, will someone teach me how to garden?"

Courtney, Deidre, Francesca, Tommy, and Sherre, all answered simultaneously, with "I will," "I would love to," "It would be a pleasure," Sure!" And, "Yes."

Kate chuckled. "Sounds like I could start looking for a plot of ground close by."

Courtney asked, "Did anyone ever hear more about that homeless man they found dead at Gypsy Clearing? There was nothing about it when I searched on the Internet." Her fingers energetically mocked typing on the dinner table.

Tom said, "Yeah. The coroner ruled it natural causes, not a homicide after all."

Deidre looked directly at Tom, "That's if 'natural causes' includes that he drank himself into a stupor at the edge of the creek and drowned in his sleep."

Tom straightened up, locked eyes with his wife, and then he looked down at his hands.

Francesca broke the resumed awkward silence, "Courtney and Tommy, are you excited about school starting soon?"

"Yes, Grandma. I am. I miss the routine."

"Not your friends?" Darian said mockingly, then he stared at the ceiling for a moment, as though needing to control some vast irritation.

Sherre jerked her head in his direction, and then restrained her anger. She kept herself from yelling, "*What's wrong with you?*" She caught Kate's expression that conveyed disgust of Darian as well. *We're kindred spirits, Kate and I.*

Tommy said, "I wish they had a class in school on how to pan for gold."

Deidre rose from the table, "I wish they had a class that taught you to volunteer to help with the dishes." She tugged on Tommy's sleeve, "Come on Tommy. It's our turn to load the dishwasher."

CHAPTER EIGHTEEN

Darian

He felt his brows come together and his eyes squint. He still remembered how odd it was when he felt slightly troubled about the collateral damage of his grandmother's accident. She died, as planned, but she killed a man when her car rammed into his truck. He decided to sooth this new, strange feeling by attending Roberto Granzella's funeral. What he hadn't expected was that Granzella's widow would be the most beautiful woman he'd ever seen in his life. He watched her hands move and her hips. He liked being in her company. Everything about her was captivating. His obsessive brain repeated, "Mine, mine, mine." She was far more beautiful than any of the women in the videos he watched to overcome his increasing inability to get sexually aroused.

From the moment he touched her hand, he knew she was the cure for his malady.

For nine months, Darian was preoccupied with taking Francesca to bed. Marrying her was a small price to pay to overcome the disorder that started after he married Julianna. He was convinced it was Julianna's fault, but after she was gone, to his frustration, even porn wasn't working.

Darian was gloating over his victory when he and Francesca left for Reno. He was exactly what Francesca's son-in-law, Tom said, "the luckiest man on earth," but he knew it had nothing to do with luck. He'd successfully enchanted this incredible, beautiful, intelligent woman, who would always know how to act; how to make him look good in any situation. However, before they left, he found himself plagued with anger over her attachment to her chickens. On their way home they had their first argument. His plan was for her to come live with him in the beautifully remodeled mansion that had belonged to his grandmother. He hated the filthy chickens. Were they more cherished than he was? Francesca assumed they would live at her ranch and she was unwilling to part with her stupid chickens. He DID NOT want the chickens at his mansion. In his stewing anger were the questions, *What if she isn't enough? Who's to say I won't end up feeling suffocated, exactly the way I did with Julianna?*

The thought of living at her ranch disgusted him. He would be constantly surrounded by that family. Those women, Sherre and Deidre, were too smart for their own good. And that teenage granddaughter was so strange, annoying, and intimidating. So serious. So intellectual. It was like she lived in a different dimension where she had more awareness than everyone else did in this one. When she looked at him he wondered if she could read his thoughts, his irritation, and his anger. He was particularly enraged around her. He would never be able to control someone like that. And, Darian was wearied by the way that boy constantly talked about finding gold. There were so many other ways to gain riches. He felt a smile tighten the muscles of his face.

Francesca tried to be nice about his performance issues, without realizing that it was all her fault. She acted as if she was embarrassed, so virginal. What a turn off. It was reminiscent of Julianna. Neither were demonstrative compared to the sexy experts on his digital screens. He had begun to resent Julianna. He could try the erectile dysfunction pills again that failed to work last time. Maybe he would start to resent Francesca too.

CHAPTER NINETEEN

The Gold Mine

Courtney accepted Tyler's invitation to go for a hike. She didn't la-la-love him, as Tommy surmised, but she liked him as a friend. Courtney knew his world revolved around video games, which caused her to feel sad.

She thought about his curly, mop-like head and how he folded his skinny arms in place like they were always somehow too long for the space they were in. It was surprising the first time she noticed his eyes were light blue. She had not noticed before, doubtless as a result of failure to look him in the eye. Eye contact with anyone was almost as difficult for her as physical contact. One time he had put his arm around her shoulder. He must have felt her stiffen, because he immediately removed it.

She knew her innate logical skills were significantly greater than her interpersonal skills. Rather than hanging out with people, she preferred music and mathematics in their unassailable world of rationality. The primary elements of Courtney's life revolved around logic. She needed a place for everything, everything in its place, and preferred everyone to be on time. Things needed to be planned and timed. Schedules that were adhered to, soothed her. She felt secure when things were predictable.

But when she heard Tyler's mom had left, she felt profound sympathy. She couldn't imagine life without her mom or her dad. They were essential to her routine and stability. She was sorry that Aunt Sherre's marriage didn't work out, but she was grateful to have her aunt nearby again. With all her misunderstandings regarding feelings and interpreting emotions, one thing she knew for sure was that it was great to be loved unconditionally by her mom, dad, grandparents, and her Aunt Sherre. They were always so accepting of her. They even seemed to be proud of her for the way she was different. She was reasonably sure the kids at school were mocking her behind her back. Her new step grandfather was beginning to mock her to her face.

Tyler told her that his father, Denny, was good to him and usually nice, but the words Tyler used to describe their relationship were, "We don't connect." Tyler had nice clothes, expensive shoes, and that mop-like hair cut was his choice at an expensive salon, not neglect. When Courtney and Tommy were invited over for pizza, they ate at a low, round table in Tyler's enormous bedroom suite. One of the rooms in this suite resembled a home theater. He had his own private bathroom and he told Courtney and Tommy that Denny's housekeeper oversaw all order and cleanliness, including Tyler's laundry.

While Courtney helped her mother pack water and snacks, Tommy inquired, "What's that for? Where are you going? Am I going too? Is that why you're making two packs?"

"Tyler and I are going out to hike this afternoon."

Tommy's face broadcasted disappointment first to Courtney, then to Deidre. He said in a melancholy tone, "I guess I'll just go play Destiny, but Tyler, my defender, won't be online."

"That is correct. He decided to get out of the house and he invited me to go hiking with him."

Deidre chuckled and said, "Tommy, one day you'll wake up and find that fantasy world is nothing like the real world."

Courtney looked up to the right, finding it hard to see how her mother would know that such information will become available at the point of waking.

Tommy continued with the slightest whine rising in his tone, "Maybe you'll find gold like Aunt Sherre and her friend, Johnny, did when they went hiking." He looked even more dejected.

Deidre smiled at Courtney. "D'you suppose Tyler would mind?"

Courtney, "I suppose not if—" She glared at Tommy. "If you even think about mocking us with your la-la—"

Tommy grinned with delight. "I won't, I won't I swear." He gave a little air punch.

Courtney slid her phone from her pocket and typed with her thumbs. Within a few seconds her phone replied with a robotic ring tone. "He says sure." She nodded at her mom. "We will need another snack pack." Tommy hugged her. She kept still and it was over quickly.

Courtney felt a hint of trepidation. She feared the complexities and emotions of the three-way interaction between her brother, Tyler, and herself may exceed her ability to interpret them, but she was determined to facilitate some authentic, fresh-air adventure for these two hardcore gamers.

Courtney said, "You are late!"

Tyler looked confused and pulled out his phone. "Only eight minutes."

"Correct." Standing at the front door, Courtney said to the kitchen door, "Bye Mom. We are leaving now." She closed the front door and handed Tyler the pack her mother had made for him. Courtney noticed his watery eyes as he examined the ziplocked pack of food and water.

Tyler put his head down and turned away quickly, tucking the bag into his backpack. "Sweet." He wiped his nose on the sleeve of his hoody. "So we're off. Which way should we go?"

"Let's stop at the Banks' residence to get permission to follow AJ Creek up on their side of the hill and use the little bridge that Mr. Banks built. Aunt Sherre told me about the bridge and a path that will lead us to a place near the creek where we will probably see a lot of toads," said Courtney.

Tommy, obviously thrilled to be part of the expedition said, "I wonder if that's where they found the gold!"

"They found gold?" This from Tyler.

"Yeah a gold nugget. Aunt Sherre has it in her room. She let me hold it."

"Maybe they found it at the old gold mine."

Tommy's voice hit a high pitch. "There's a gold mine?"

"Yeah. You don't know about the old gold mine?"

"No! I wonder why Dad never told me!"

"It is not difficult to calculate the reasons. It is probably because he was afraid you'd decide to move there," said Courtney.

"Oh no," said Tyler, "You wouldn't want to move there. It was gross five years ago. It's probably grosserific now. My dad drove us up a gravel road from Brandt Road, but I think we can get there going up the Banks' side of the hill following the creek. On the Brandt Road side, it's blocked off with a chain when it gets to the mine. I remember seeing a lot of signs, but I don't remember what they said."

Tommy could barely control his enthusiasm. "Gosh! I wonder if there are signs on this side to help us find it and find some gold!"

Attempting to bring practical reality back into the conversation, Courtney said. "How about we see how we feel after we climb to Toad Haven?"

The smooth, fallen log was right where Courtney expected to find it and Aunt Sherre was right about the spot she had named Toad

Haven. There were more little toads than they'd ever seen in their lives. The children sat in the shade, ate their snacks and drank some water. All the while, Tommy incessantly worked to convince Courtney and Tyler that the hill above wasn't that all that steep. After they'd rested, his reasoning finally prevailed.

They noticed thick underbrush ahead. They grabbed protruding branches and balanced on toppled logs and large rocks to cross the creek acrobatically. Tyler gallantly assisted Courtney, but Tommy kept his mouth zipped as he promised. He slipped once and totally drenched his left pant leg up to his calf. He laughed at the squeaky suction of his tennis shoe, not realizing it wouldn't be funny later when it would be important to be dry.

All three were entirely breathless when they reached a flat clearing at the top of the ridge. As they pulled out water bottles, the ground beneath them started to wobble. Courtney's water splashed her chin and she felt the cool water on her chest, wetting her T-shirt. She capped the bottle quickly and stuffed it into her backpack pocket. Tyler's bottle flew out of his hand and rolled away, then started to roll back, and then rolled away again. What they intuitively did next, probably saved their lives. As the ground swayed, they put their arms out as if they were flying, but then they looked at each other and instinctively drew together, wrapping arms under each other's backpacks into a group hug. Courtney was amazed that in this crisis, her human body repulsion reflex did not activate.

The spot where they stood stayed level as the sinkhole collapsed around them. At first it was as if they were in an elevator, plummeting at an unreasonable speed, then their slab of wood hit bottom with a thud. Still clinging to each other, they were tossed into heap. Courtney and Tommy landed violently on top of Tyler which forced a noise out of him, similar to a shriek. The table tilted and they began roll over onto Courtney, then Tommy, and then they came to a stop on top of poor Tyler once again. Courtney extracted herself from the huddle and put her hands onto the splintery board beneath them to help her stand up. She grabbed Tommy's hand and helped him to his feet. Debris was tumbling down around them. They could barely see each other through the landslide of dirt and dust. Tommy and Courtney bent to help Tyler up just in time. He moaned loudly when they pulled each of his arms, but he was able to stand. When Tommy released one of Tyler's arms, he used it to grab his side and said, "Ouch, ouch, ouch, ouch." Still holding Tyler's arm, Courtney grabbled Tommy's hand and pulled them back to the center of the wooden platform, on which they'd just ridden down, into the dark pit. An avalanche of dirt dropped onto the spot where they had lain. The ground beneath them shifted slightly for several more seconds, and then it was quiet except for the sound of settling earth. They embraced again in an emotional, filthy, frantic group hug. Courtney once again disconnected herself from their cluster, pulled out her phone, and initiated the flashlight app. The table-top-like platform that saved them was wedged into dirt walls on three sides, but the fourth side dropped off into a yawning crevasse of deep, dark oblivion. Courtney involuntarily shivered when she realized the light could not find the bottom of the cavity. She stepped back closer to the boys and the center of their table. The steep, newly-formed, unclimbable walls that surrounded them were still steadily sifting dust. It would be impossible to climb to safety.

Courtney pulled her water bottle out of her pocket, grateful that it survived their plunge into darkness. She sorrowfully remembered Tyler's water bottle rolling away. "Tommy?"

Tommy's voice reflected his despair, "Yeah."

"Can you check to see if you still have water?"

The light from her phone revealed the filthy statue that was her brother and the bushy-topped figure that resembled her friend, Tyler. Courtney knew, even without a mirror that she also looked like a lumpy pile of dirt. She started to giggle, which was rare for her. Tyler and Tommy started giggling too, but Tyler grabbed his side screamed, "Ow," and then he started to cry, which triggered the same from Tommy and Courtney. They had rivulets of mud forming on their faces. Courtney checked for a cellular signal, just in case. Of course, there was none. They were in a deep dark hole within a Black Hole. The sliver of light above them was disappearing. It would be pitch dark soon.

They reached for each other as the floor once again began to wobble.

CHAPTER TWENTY

Rescue for Hire

Tom's text message ringtone went off. "It's from Deidre. She's in a panic. The kids haven't come home yet."

Sherre looked at Kate. They halted their disinfecting process, left the olive oil jugs soaking in the millroom deep sink, and followed Tom out the door; out of the cellular Black Hole. Sherre heard herself exhale although she hadn't been aware she was holding her breath.

They stayed near as he walked in circles with his phone held high. When the signal came in, he called his wife. "Yeah. That's a long time. Call the Sheriff and tell him we're going to start searching. They might not get here for a while and it's going to get dark soon. Let's start searching without them." He nodded as he listened. "He is? Good. Have him come with you. Let's meet at the old barn." He held the phone away from his face for a minute and said to Sherre and Kate, "Denny's there. He was looking for Tyler."

"Wait! Don't hang up!" Sherre interrupted. "Tell them to meet us at Johnny's—at the house. Tell them to bring a piece of each kid's dirty laundry. I think I know where they may have gone. There's a gold mine above the Banks' Estate. Tommy—"

Tom's eyes widened, he nodded nervously and said into the phone. "Right, right. Deidre, you and Denny meet us at the Banks'. Did you hear Sherre? Yeah something they've worn. Okay." He waited. "Perfect. Okay, okay. See you there." He clicked off his phone. "Denny's got one of Tyler's hoodies in his truck." He pulled a face that looked like he'd just smelled something unpleasant, "I'm sure Deidre can find some dirty laundry. They'll be on their way in a minute or two."

Kate and Sherre slid into the passenger side of Tom's truck. Sherre barely got the door closed before Tom's sudden acceleration tore up the gravel as they headed down the hill. Sherre had her phone at the ready and pushed a button. "Johnny. We need you and Marcus. The kids left for a hike this morning and—oh gosh. There you are. Tom stop. I'll ride with Johnny and fill him in."

Tom pulled his truck up next to Johnny's. Sherre dropped onto the gravel as soon as the truck halted. She tapped the truck twice loudly as soon as she closed the door.

Johnny hurried to politely open his truck door for her. Marcus impolitely ambled ahead of her to take the middle seat. Before she had a chance to hoist herself up, Johnny lifted her onto the seat that had been warmed by the slanting sun. She used the precious saved seconds to call her mom. She smiled at Johnny as he closed the truck door. "Mom! Please pray. The kids are missing. Tyler Garter is with them. Yeah, we felt it in the millroom. It was such a minor earthquake, we didn't think much of it, but you're right—if it was centered wherever they are—oh gosh. This could be so much worse that I thought." Her heart was pounding. Her hand was shaking. Johnny must have noticed. He reached across Marcus to gently pat her on the shoulder. "Yeah. Deidre called the Sheriff, but we're not waiting for them. Kate's in Tom's truck. We were in the millroom, but they dropped me at my house. I'm with Johnny and his bloodhound." She felt the comfort of Marcus' warm body beside her on the seat and leaned against it. "Deidre's with Denny. We're meeting at the Banks'. Yeah, the house. It's closest to the old gold mine. You know how Tommy's been so obsessed with gold—sure. Okay. We'll wait for you, but don't take too long. I know you. No need to make coffee and sandwiches. And do NOT take time to put on lipstick or refresh your make-up. This is a 'come as you are' search party." Sherre giggled. "Yes, Mom, you can grab a case of water. That'd be great. See you in a few minutes, very few! Okay?"

Johnny maneuvered his truck through the other two in his driveway and pulled into his garage, leaving room for Darian's Cadillac. Johnny hurried to get Sherre's door, but she didn't give him a chance. This time, Marcus waited politely to follow Sherre out the passenger side. The truck engine ticked itself to sleep.

As Sherre approached the gathering crowd, the first thing Sherre noticed was Denny standing nervously twisting Tyler's hoodie. A half-moon of dampness showed on the pale blue cloth beneath his armpits. His attention was fully focused on Kate.

Kate returned his gaze, but was the first to turn her eyes away.

Sherre said to everyone, "Mom's on the way. She promised to get here quickly. Hi Lois!"

Lois stepped out of her front door and stood above them on her porch. She waved to Sherre, but then her questioning face sought Johnny's.

Johnny leaped up the two steps and put his arm tenderly around his mom. "Kids are missing. Probably went up there." He pointed up the hill. "We're going to find them." He smiled reassuringly at her, but Sherre could detect a faint strain around his eyes.

Lois nodded at her son. "That's the way they went."

"You saw them?"

"They knocked on the door this afternoon and asked permission to hike on our property." She looked at Tom and Deidre. "Great kids you've got there. Very polite." She turned back to face Johnny and put her hands together into a position of prayer.

Johnny knowingly smiled at her. "I'll call you as soon as I have a signal. Right now, we need the first aid kit, flashlights, a couple of towels, and a few blankets. If you can get those and pass them around for us to carry, I'll grab some rope from the shop." He kissed his mother on the forehead, bounded down the porch steps, and ran down the hill to the shop. Marcus stayed at his heels.

Denny ran with them for several steps and explained to Johnny, "I've got a tactical flashlight, a small blanket, and some ratcheted tie downs in the RAM." When he returned from his truck, he shifted all the objects onto his left arm, approached Kate, and used his right hand to tilt his Stenson.

"Kate, this is Denny Garter. Denny, Kate Stryker." Sherre watched with amusement as they awkwardly greeted each other and touched hands.

"Your son. You must be so worried."

Denny nodded like a bobble head that had been barely jiggled into bobbling, keeping both his nod and his emotions tightly constrained. His eyes got shiny. "You never think—did you feel the earthquake?"

"Yes. We felt it in the millroom." Kate reached out to briefly rest on his forearm. "They may be fine, but just unable to cross back onto the path home … or something."

Johnny returned with the rope draped diagonally across his body like commando ammunition. Bunched into his large hands were the dark green T-shirt and a pair of turquoise running shorts Deidre had given him. "May I have that?"

"Sure." Denny shifted a blanket and handed Johnny the twisted hoodie. "Good idea Banks." He turned to Kate, "Would you mind holding these a minute?" He handed her the blanket and the flashlight, and then began to coiling the tie down straps so he could drape them commando style.

"Come here boy." Johnny squatted to hold the clothes close to Marcus' nose. "We need to find these kids." Then, he patiently explained to the dog, "We want to stick with you though, so help me hang on, okay?" He caressed the dog's neck with his free hand. "No running ahead this time." Johnny looked up with relief at the sound of the Cadillac barreling up the hill.

Sherre was smiling at the conversation between dog and man. Her phone rang with a Screaming Horror ringtone. She noticed Johnny chuckling. "Chuck. I don't have time right now." She hated that she heard her voice crack and that she saw her hand shaking. "No. I can't. We're in the middle of a crisis." She paused to listen. "Seriously? I told you not now. It can't be as important as this. My niece, nephew, and Denny's kid are missing. I'll get back to you later. Yeah. Okay. Okay. We're about to go into a Black Hole so I can't. Right. If I remember." Her phone slipped onto the ground instead of into her pocket. Johnny picked it up and handed it to her. "Thanks." She realized everyone was staring at her. She pressed a pair of fingertips to her throbbing temple and consciously tried to change her expression. She shrugged at Deidre, who had come alongside to give her a sideways hug. Sherre's voice was shaky. "He says he needs to talk to me." She felt her face flush with heat. She pressed her fist firmly into the center of her upper chest. "Well, um," She looked around, said, "Forget him. Let's go." She nodded at Johnny.

Johnny was straining to hold Marcus back. "Hold on boy. Marcus wants to go this way." Marcus had his snout close to the ground. Pulling at the leash, he began to tow Johnny up the hill. "Mom was right."

Sherre noticed tension between Francesca and Darian as they were hurriedly handing out water. Everything about Darian seemed to be clenched. He seemed agitated. He was pale, his skin slick with sweat. There was a round patch of sweat on the front of his shirt. Sherre took two bottles from her mother's hands and jogged to catch up with Johnny. "Of course she was."

Johnny briefly turned from the taut leash to look at Sherre. He looked perplexed.

"Your mom. You said your mom was right. Your mom's always right." She smiled.

As the path narrowed above the Banks' house, the party fell into pairs. Deidre and Tom were directly behind Johnny and Sherre. Kate paired up with Denny behind them. Darian and Francesca followed in the rear.

Straight up a steep incline, they followed a well-worn path that led them to the small wooden bridge that Johnny's dad built many years before so they could conveniently cross AJ Creek to the less overgrown west side. Thick bushes and brambles on the east side of the creek bent down to the water as if they were drinking from their branches, not just their roots. The searchers continued to climb at a steady pace until Marcus perked up with excitement and pulled Johnny ahead to the log where Johnny and Sherre had often sat studying tadpoles. "I think they sat here," said Johnny. Marcus continued momentarily, crisscrossing the area before pointing his nose across the creek and plunged both front feet into the water, again straining the leash. "Okay. Good boy. Just *wait* a second." Marcus backed up and sat obediently on the deep grass at the edge of the creek, but he was twitchy and anxious to advance. His silky, ivory coat trembled in anticipation. "The kids must have used those rocks and branches as stepping stones and crossed here." He grinned the familiar mischievous grin that Sherre remembered well. "They probably got wet."

"And they probably didn't care." Sherre smiled back.

"I've got waterproof boots on so I'll follow Marcus the way he wants to go, but first I'll hold up those branches above the path so you can stay on this side for a while. They're thick right here, but then there's a cleared path all of the way up to the water tower. There's one on the east side too. We'll both need to veer away from the creek and then weave back again, but there are obstacles and paths that make the direction obvious. Do you remember the short crossing up there? Just before you get to the water tower?"

Sherre nodded.

"Do you mind leading the others that way? I'll meet up with you there."

Sherre remembered, now, how steep the climb was. Brambles and huge rocks forced them to hike in a zigzag pattern, which made the trip twice as long, but also alleviated the steepness of the rise. Each arduous step brought her closer to Johnny, who she knew would arrive first, where the creek met up with water tower. And he did. He was waiting patiently on the other side. Marcus not so much. He tugged impatiently, nose to the ground, first to the right, then to the left. Johnny looked down at his phone and called across as soon as the others were in earshot, "Does anyone have a signal?"

They all pulled out their phones to check.

"Marcus is definitely leading us in the direction of the abandoned gold mine. There's an old gravel road that goes there. It comes up from Brandt Road at the curve where it bends from east to northeast. If we could let the men from the sheriff's department know where we are and where Marcus is leading us, they could come up that way."

Darian was walking around in circles holding his phone in front of his face. "Right here! I've got two bars if I hold it here." He was pointing southeast, holding the phone a foot above his head.

Francesca beamed with pride. "Deidre. Do you have the Sheriff's direct line still in your phone?"

"Yeah here." Deidre walked over to Darian.

Johnny said, "We're going to keep moving. Follow us straight up the hill from that side. There's a shorter crossing up ahead."

Sherre nodded and turned to give the others a chance to catch up. She smiled when she noticed that, though the path was wider, Denny and Kate stayed side by side. Tom had waited for Deidre. They were holding hands. Francesca and Darian, however, were not. Unmistakably, things were strained. Sherre saw something resolute in Darian's face, something private and determined and deeply terrifying. Francesca's expression was brave, but hurt, possibly confused.

The climb from Toad Haven to the water tower had been steep, but the next segment of the path was even more extreme. Sherre found herself breathless. At the brow of the ridge, on a sloping plateau, as promised, once again Johnny waited on the other side of the creek. There was nothing patient about Marcus. His flat nose zigzagged across the ground repeatedly and he yanked at the leash. Johnny calmed him by praising him, and then bent down to hug him and talk softy. Sherre watched Johnny's hand retrieve a treat from his pocket that Marcus accepted into his mouth. His other end whipped its mighty tail.

The creek was narrower at the location Johnny had chosen, but it was still tricky to cross. Johnny commanded Marcus to lie down and stay, then he reached across the water for Sherre's hand, pulling her safely to the other side. Sherre sat down on a large rock alongside of Marcus and absentmindedly began caressing one of his ears. Johnny helped Denny across, and then Denny reached out to assist each of the others. Johnny sat for a moment next to

Sherre. Each of them took a moment to rest and guzzle water.

Johnny stood up and said to the searchers. "Ready to move forward?" Marcus bounded to his feet, placed his snout on the ground, and wagged his tail zealously, but stood obediently in the spot where he had been commanded to stay. "Okay Boy, lead the way."

The path was clear, but steep. Sherre noticed Marcus' increased excitement. She turned and said to the others, "Come on, I know it's hard, but I think we're almost there. Marcus just pulled Johnny over the top of that hill.

Marcus abruptly stopped and backed up using his powerful hind feet to pull himself back from the edge. His front paws had begun to slip into the soft earth. Johnny turned to the search party that had just crested the top of the plateau. He held up his hand and called out, "Stay back! There's a sinkhole."

Sherre clasped her hand over face, "Oh no! Do you think the kids—"

Courtney's voice beneath her in the darkness cried out, "Aunt Sherre?"

"Oh Courtney. Are you hurt? Where's Tommy? Is Tyler there? Is everyone okay?"

Deidre came alongside Sherre, "Mom's here, honey, so is Dad. We'll get you out of there." Her shaky voice was not convincing.

Courtney called up, "Tommy and I are okay, but Tyler's hurt and the last roll took him to the edge of our board. Tommy's trying to hold onto him. I'm trying to hold onto Tommy."

Johnny zoomed his flashlight in circles and spotted a stack of old lumber. He wedged the light into the crook of a tree to illuminate their work area. He started dragging boards to the edge of the hole, placing them side by side, perpendicular to the sinkhole. Everyone, except Darian, followed Johnny's lead and strategically placed their flashlights around the area to light the region. Denny and Tom caught onto Johnny's plan immediately. They pitched in. A firm platform at the edge of the sinkhole started to materialize. Marcus stood to the side, away from the growing activity, pointing his mighty nose and directing his full attention toward the children in the hole. Johnny and Denny stopped momentarily to dump their blankets and ropes at Sherre and Deidre's feet. Kate, Sherre, and Deidre started rolling large rocks to the end of the boards to give the platform stability. Denny found, and moved, a few cinder blocks for further reinforcement. Francesca and Darian had stepped away from the working crew. They settled to the left where the ground seemed to be more solid. It was veined with roots from a nearby tree. Between their perch and the children's table lay the cavernous darkness that Courtney's phone flashlight had revealed to her earlier. Darian flashed his light into the hole. The children were lying down on their stomachs lined up side by side, Tommy had removed his backpack and was in the middle. Both Tommy and Courtney were hanging onto Tyler. Courtney's arms stretched across her little brother. She had wrapped a strap from Tyler's backpack around her wrist. Tommy had a grip on Tyler's belt.

"Good!" Johnny called to Darian, "Thanks. The light helps, but be careful, you're standing above a deep gap. It looks like they're on a portion of the roof to the old mine." Darian moved his light to the five-foot wide cavity beneath the spot where Darian and Francesca stood. The blackness beyond absorbed the light.

"Hang on." said Tom to the children. "I'll come get you."

CHAPTER TWENTY-ONE

Emergency

Johnny MacGyvered a harness from Denny's tie down straps and cushioned it with a towel. He expertly secured the tie downs to his rope and wrapped the other end of the rope around the nearest strong tree trunk. Tom secured himself into the harness, and then stood at the edge of the sinkhole facing Johnny, Denny, Kate, Deidre, and Sherre, who were lined up on the makeshift landing, holding the rope attached to his harness. Tom repelled backward over the side.

The flashlight wavered in Darian's hand when they heard the emergency vehicles' sirens below the ridge. Sherre glanced toward Darian when she saw the movement. It was as if he was hollowed out and coiled like a spring. The light danced as he began to pace several steps away from Francesca, and then return to where she stood rooted, completely focused on the trapped children.

Two fireman, three sheriff deputies, and four paramedics bounded up the hill. The ground trembled beneath their boots. Johnny waved and called to them. He directed them to take a longer route that was less likely to disturb the fragile earth surrounding the sinkhole. They circled and scrambled up the hill on the same side from which the search party had come. As Tom perched solidly onto the kid's wooden table, dust and debris slithered down on top of them. He had pounced down to the table, and then lay down so he could spread his body and arms across the children. Rocks and dirt plummeted onto his back. The pressure of Tom's landing caused Tyler to yelp. Those holding the rope were able to relax momentarily.

When the flashlight in his hand stopped twitching, Sherre and Kate turned their attention to Darian. He was smiling at Francesca, but his smile was eerie, like reflection on water, distorted and illusory. Nervous energy was radiating off of him. Kate dropped the rope and dashed toward him. Francesca was startled away from her absorption in Tom's recuse attempt. She jerked around in time to see Kate slide onto her belly and tackle Darian at the knees. Kate's tackle foiled Darian's attempt to push Francesca into the dark abyss. Francesca took a step back from the slipping earth. Darian's expression was sheer panic as he teetered on the chasm's edge.

Kate grabbed his ankles, but his falling weight dragged her down behind him as he fell. Denny bolted from the rope and threw himself on top of Kate, landing on the back of her legs. The top half of her body was sloping into the pit. He wrapped his arms around her waist. Francesca grabbed the belt on Denny's pants and began, with amazing strength, to pull Denny and Kate through the dirt until most of Kate's body was back on solid ground. Kate's head and arms still hung over the edge. Darian was lost into the blackness below.

CHAPTER TWENTY-TWO

Aftermath

It was strangely quiet after the two ambulances pulled away, one with Tyler and Denny, the other with Courtney and Tommy. Deidre, Tom, and Kate followed them to the hospital in a sheriff's cruiser.

Sherre sat next to her mother in the back seat of the other cruiser, still parked at the bottom of the gold mine property. A sickening ache filled her head. Both cruiser doors were open to let in the cool evening breeze. Someone had considerately wrapped her mother in a blanket. Johnny and Marcus had returned to the sinkhole to see if they could help with the unlikely recovery of Darian's body.

Behind Francesca's eyes swirled the gray tears of anxiety and sadness. "If Kate hadn't stopped him, he would have killed me. I knew he seemed angry the past few days and I couldn't figure out why, but I had no idea he hated me so much."

"I don't think he hated you, Mom." Sherre considered her words carefully and decided it would all come out anyway. Maybe it would help Francesca get through this confusion if she heard the truth now. "Believe it or not, I don't think it was about you at all."

"What do you mean? Of course it was. He was going to push me into that pit!"

"Before Kate left for the hospital, she told me that she's been worried ever since Darian convinced you to elope, that he would try to kill you."

"Oh my Lord!" Francesca put her hand over her heart. "No! Why?"

"There's no evidence, but Kate's sure he's murdered before and made the murders look like accidents."

"So he is a serial killer?"

"Seems so. I think he was motivated by money the first couple of times. Kate thinks he still has money, but he was either trying to increase his assets, or, how creepy is this? She thinks he got caught up in the thrill of murdering and getting away with it."

"What a fiend! I married a fiend!" Her hand remained on her chest, protectively covering her heart. Tears poured from her eyes.

"Yeah. So scary." She patted her mother's hand that clasped the blanket.

"I despise myself for being so gullible."

"No despising. Not allowed." Sherre's eyes glistened. "I'm *so* glad I didn't lose you, Mom." She scooted closer to her mother. They hugged until they were startled apart by the cruiser rocking violently. Both doors began to close. Sherre thrust both feet out and stopped the door on her side and prevented it from locking them in. "That was the worst so far!" They sat up abruptly and looked at each other in fear. Sherre whispered to herself, "Johnny."

Sherre studied the shadows emerging from under the dark trees until she recognized his walk. If she had any doubt, as soon as Johnny came into the moonlight, she saw Marcus at this side. She bolted to meet him. "Is everyone okay?"

"Yeah, well, everyone that went back is okay. We set up the balance rig on the firm side of the hole that had woven roots. That fireman named Jerry has rock climbing and spelunking experience so he volunteered to repel down to see if Darian was still alive. But thank God, before he got close to the edge, he backed off and we all backed up." He chuckled a brief machinegun chuckle. "You felt it, right?"

Sherre nodded with her eyes wide. "Of course! What's funny?"

"When the ground started rocking, we all clutched the tree trunk at one place or another. It was an intimate moment. We probably looked like the bundle of soldiers lifting the American flag at Iwo Jima, except it was a wobbly tree instead of a flag that centered us. From where I was, I could see the table that held up the kids. It swayed until it dropped into the hole where Darian fell, then the three other walls, except for the one that held our tree, collapsed in on top of it. If Darian was alive before—" Johnny shook his head slowly, and then said quietly. "He's buried under tons of dirt, Sherre." He took a deep breath. "The firemen have called off the rescue because the sinkhole is too unstable. Darian's body will never be recovered. The Sheriff will be cordoning this entire area off." He waved his arm in a broad circle.

Speechless and overcome with emotion, Sherre shivered.

He drew back and looked at her searchingly, then he put his arms around her and pulled her into his chest. "Are you okay?"

Her voice muffled against his chest, "Thank God you got the kids out—that table. I wonder what held it up when the kids and Tom were on it."

Johnny vibrated with a machinegun chuckle, "Four guardian angels."

Sherre giggled. "No doubt. One for each person and one for each corner."

"Shall we go tell your mom about Darian together?"

"Thanks Johnny. I'll hold her. You tell her."

Chapter Twenty-Three

Victoria's Secret

Sherre fell back on her bed and stared at the ceiling. Her head still ached as she recalled the dreadful day. She was exhausted, as if she'd gone days without food and water, but there was also a sensation of hope, or perhaps a release, as though a bird had just flown free after being trapped in a dark box. She'd done a full day's work that started at 6:30 that morning, and then she'd suffered the past five hours of terror... She said out loud to her digital clock, "Only ten thirty?"

She needed to sleep, but she knew that wasn't happening until she processed something that was nagging at her from a back corner of her brain. What she felt seemed unbearable, but she wasn't sure what it was. Her analytical mind went to work on each thought and tested them against the feeling in her gut. It wasn't the kids. She was sure they were okay and that they'd bounce back from their traumatic experience. An uneasiness was following her, as though there was a shadow behind her and if she stopped moving the shadow just waited. It wasn't that her stepfather, a serial killer, had died trying to kill her mother. That thought, though disturbing, was laced with feelings of ironic satisfaction; karma; payback; and peace. Only Kate had suspected Francesca was in real danger. Now, Mom no longer was. *Thank God for Kate!* Even after the Sheriff took their statements and Francesca positively reported that she saw Darian's arms extended, ready to push her, her mother still appeared unable to accept what they all saw clearly. Sherre tucked Francesca into her bed and sat with her until she drowsily said, "What if he thought I was falling and he was trying—"

Sherre allowed her mom to fall asleep in a state of denial. Her mother saw and heard what happened. She would work it out when her raw emotions allowed her to accept the wretched truth. Sherre's body resisted her first effort to roll off the bed as if she weighed a few hundred pounds and she was attached to it by glue. She knew she'd feel better after a much-needed bath so she tried again. The vibration in her pocket, accompanied by the Screaming Horror ring tone startled her. Her heart and body jumped. Wearily, she said, "Chuck. It's ten-thirty. Whatever it is, it can't be that important."

"It is. You said you'd call me back and you didn't. And now I just saw on the news, your mother's husband died in a sinkhole?"

"Yes, but the kids are okay."

"Good. Good. Yeah, they said the kids were okay too. I was relieved to hear it. Denny's kid is the only one that needs to stay overnight in the hospital, right? They didn't say the names of the kids, but they showed Deidre and Tom ushering two kids out. They digitized the kid's faces."

She knew him so well. If it weren't such a good reason for him to seem sincerely concerned, she'd have assumed this was one of his manipulative ploys that traditionally preceded an emotional punch in the stomach, and she would have asked, *"What do you really want, Chuck?"* Instead, she waited. And she knew. This is it. This is what had been gnawing at her soul. Chuck said he needed to talk to her and her subconscious was unwilling to face this conversation, just as her mother's subconscious was unwilling to believe her husband had tried to kill her. Her heart hurt when Sherre realized she wished she could talk to her dad. He was so wise and he knew her better than anyone. When Sherre brought her problems to him, he always knew what she should do. What would he say if she told him about Chuck? About Victoria? About the recent manipulative lies and seduction? She took a deep breath, tried to clear her mind, and pictured herself standing in the millroom pouring her story out to her dad. What would he say? His answer came to her clearly, *"Beware Sweetheart. Chuck Shockley is so charming."* She needed to heal from Chuck's rejection; her sense of failure; her vulnerability; her failed marriage. She wasn't ready to tear off the emotional scab. Oh Daddy, *I was so sure it would last until death do us part. One life. One marriage. Failure was not an option.* She'd made two vows. The one to Chuck the day she married him. The other was to herself, long before her wedding day. She was certain she would never be a victim of divorce, but if she was wrong, if it didn't work out, she vowed to never remarry. And now, insult to injury, what Kate aptly called "the double-edge sword of feminism" that gave her an opportunity to become the self-reliant, successful fixer she was, also gave him the right to alimony. Her father's effectual advice to always ask herself, "What do I know for sure?" had propelled her through tough assessments of other people's situations, but was failing her in her own. The only thing she was sure of was that she was full of anger, and she knew her anger would veil the clarity of her thinking. *Do I still love him? How could I have ever loved him?* She hated this. She had zero control in this situation or of her own emotions. She remembered her dad quoting Winston Churchill, who defined success as: The ability to go from failure to failure without losing enthusiasm. *Well I seem to have the failures down, but I've definitely lost my enthusiasm.*

Chuck interrupted her thoughts, "Sherre, are you still there?"

She sighed, "Yes."

"I need to see you, Sherre."

"I'm not falling for that again, Chuck. I've started locking my doors. Is that why you are calling? Did you try to come in when I wasn't here? You're not welcome here."

"No, I know. I'm at the Garter Saloon. Come see me."

"I'm tired, Chuck. More than tired. I'm sick and tired of your lies and manipulation."

"Please, Sherre. I need to talk to you. I have something to tell you."

"So tell me."

"Not on the phone. Has to be face to face. I know you think I'm a villain, but I'm not. I have a heart. Really, I do. This is important and I'm here, in town. I promise it won't take long and you'll be glad you didn't wait for a different day when you—"

"Okay, okay!" She wasn't sure if she was more frustrated with him or her own inability to say no to him. "I need a shower. Give me a half an hour."

The thought of meeting Chuck was like a stick that poked her with each heartbeat, a familiar stab somewhere near her solar plexus. Why? What does he want? She finished buttoning her plaid shirt, glanced into the mirror, and patted her pale cheeks, hoping to revive the color that even a hot shower failed to renew. She screwed up her unmade-up face into an angry and mean look, and then stuck her tongue out at the reflection. Then she took a breath and returned to an expression which she hoped was demure, with a taste of arrogance. She marched out to her car with a mantra for every step, "Jerk, jerk, jerk, jerk."

Chuck waved to her from the corner booth, and then he stood up to move to the opposite side of the table. He disappeared from her view behind the tall, mahogany-colored partition.

When Sherre came around the wall, Victoria came into view, sitting beside Chuck, possessively holding his arm. Sherre said, "Really? Did you invite me here to make me sick to my stomach?" And she did feel sick; her stomach was hot, her mouth felt coated with acrid bile. She may need to excuse herself to barf in the bathroom. She needed water and had a strong desire to brush her teeth or swish strong mouthwash. Sherre turned to Brenna Williams, the longtime Garter cocktail waitress, who was hovering not far from the booth, apparently trying to catch what was going on without being obvious about it. "Hi Brenna, Could you please bring me some ice water with a straw?" Sherre sat down. The booth was permeated with the mingled smell of Chuck's aftershave, Victoria's perfume, and the tequila shot on the table in front of Chuck. "So what's this, Chuck? Did you bring Victoria to insult me further? Or, do you want her privy to the ruthless traitor side of you?" She looked directly into Victoria's catlike, made up eyes. "See what you're getting into?" Then focusing back on Chuck, she said, "What is it now? Are you going to ask for the house, *plus* alimony?"

"Well, um, sort of, but not exactly." He picked up the shot glass and downed it one gulp. He lifted it toward Brenna, who was no longer bothering to fake interest in their conversation.

Sherre considered asking Brenna to join them in the booth, thinking she may have the comfort of an ally, but then she was distracted when her leg suddenly began to jerk uncontrollably. She hoped Chuck and Victoria hadn't noticed. She pressed down hard on it beneath the table with her hand. With her other hand, she gratefully accepted the water from Brenna without giving Brenna a chance to set it down. She drank so quickly and deeply, it generated a brain freeze. "So what is this about exactly, besides torture?"

"Victoria's pregnant."

Sherre had the physical sensation of the water draining straight down through her body, through her feet, and then out through the floor.

A small noise erupted out of Brenna that sounded similar to a hiccup.

Sherre stared down at the table so intently that she was startled by Chuck's gentle touch on her chin forcing her to look up. She was so close to tears she didn't move except that her left knee continued to tremble in a bouncing motion. She glanced at Victoria first, and then stared into Chuck's dark eyes and saw something she never expected: understanding. She saw a muscle twitch at the corner of his left eye.

"I know. I'm sorry. I really am." He downed another shot, and slurred his words, "You said I'm ruthless, but you are wrong. I'm not intentionally cruel, Sherre. I didn't mean for any of this to happen. I wasn't trying to hurt you."

Her face felt hot. She heard nastiness come through in her tone, "So what now? You want me to give you the house so you, Victoria, and your baby can live happily ever after on my alimony checks?"

"No." His hand was shaking as he lifted Victoria's water glass with a nod to her. He drank. "I'm going to marry Victoria right away. As soon as our divorce is final. There won't be any alimony. We would like to keep the house though. We'll buy you out."

Victoria sat smugly smiling at Sherre.

Sherre had never seen Victoria smile before and she realized she knew nothing about this woman, whom she'd only met that one time in Sherre's kitchen after she'd spent the night in Sherre's bed with Sherre's husband. She may still need to excuse herself to vomit. It hadn't occurred to Sherre that Victoria Sanders may have money or resources or even her own life, since she had seemingly, successfully stolen Sherre's. "I see."

"Bruce, my lawyer says, if you'll agree to everything, we can do this really fast." He patted Victoria's hand that was still clutching his arm. "Brooosh said he can do a 'Pro se filing,' or something like that. The tequila was beginning to greatly affect his pronunciation. "We amicably divorce and he can probably take it to the court for us within a week or two after we sign the papers. We don't even have to go to court with him. He'll go to court for us and just take the am-ick-a-bleee signed papers." He pleadingly looked across the table, his eyebrows drawn together thoughtfully, as though he was considering something he had not thought he would be called upon to consider. "Sherre. Please."

"Okay."

CHAPTER TWENTY-FOUR

Help Me

Sherre dropped to her knees by her bed, put her face into her hands and took several deep breaths. She felt unworthy, as usual, to talk to God. She was also experiencing a kind of mental paralysis that occurred whenever she tried to pray. Her exhaustion almost prevailed, but her head snapped forward and shocked her back to alertness. At last she said, "Okay Jesus. Here I am. As you know, I'm not good at this. It's probably because I don't do it often enough. I need you to help me."

Sherre started by filling Him in on everything that was happening to her just in case He didn't know that Victoria was pregnant. Unable to bring up Darian and admit to Jesus she was glad he was dead; that she was relieved he was no longer a threat to her mom, she instead thanked Him that the kids, her mom, and Johnny were safe. She reminded Him of how she'd tried so hard all of her life to be a good person and do things well. She folded her hands and lifted her eyes to heaven in a traditional prayer pose and began to speak out loud, "I don't know if mom is getting any money, but if she is it will be a long time before she gets it. It won't be here in time to pay the balloon payment. And you know how reliable Chuck is. Even if he keeps his word to buy me out of the house that will probably also take a long time. Do you want us to lose our property? I'm sorry, that was impertinent.

"I know that some things are not for me to see or know. My marriage, God, is gone for sure now. And Tom and Deedee. Are they going to break up too? Can you help them? Can you help me?"

She quit talking. She wasn't sure why she did or what would happen next. If God was going to answer her prayers, she realized it could take time. Time, time, time. She didn't have time. That's why she was asking. They were running out of time. Then, to her amazement, she got an immediate answer. She didn't hear a voice, but she received an impression so strong, she knew it was the answer—

"No."

For a moment she was stunned. She felt her blood leave her face so rapidly, it may have left an indentation in her temples. She pondered why God would say, "No." Why would He ignore her cry for help when she felt so helpless? Everything was going wrong and she couldn't fix it, but she had tried so hard. Was He angry with her for failing in her marriage? She certainly was. Incriminating self-talk filled her head daily. She pondered and prayed longer, but her prayers were mostly without words and she didn't get any more impressions or answers. She questioned herself and her motives. She accusingly questioned God, but then realized who she was talking to, and apologized. In a sense of surrender she again spoke out loud, "No, you won't help me." She laid her head down onto her comfortable bed, and in her exhaustion, she dozed off.

She felt a warm, comforting grasp take her hand and lift her up. He was guiding her through an open meadow. A fragrance of sweet flowers surrounded her in a soft, swirling breeze. They walked at first, but then they began to run faster and faster, both of them giggling as they approached what she knew was a treasure. He smiled at her and nodded. "Yes, for where your treasure is, there your heart will be also." A pillar of wind rose before them, a source of sweet smelling aroma that engulfed her. A shadow, edged with the yearnings of her heart, beckoned her to return to the perpetual, self-determined aspects of her physical world. There were two, distinct life forces: one propelling her forward to something that frightened her because it was unknown and unnerving; the other, was the comfortable shadow. But she felt brave and willing to go forward because she was not alone. A mist came up from the ground. A double rainbow ahead of them arched over a path that appeared before them. She turned to Him and spoke with her mind, "Is it the Treasure?" He nodded. "The Treasure of Heaven?" He smiled, chuckled and nodded again. It occurred to her at the moment how He was so full of joy. She had read and been taught, of course, that joy was part of the essence of God, but she never pondered how joyful He was; how she would be so entirely filled with joy as she held His hand and walked with Him. She knew the Treasure she had discovered was the comprehensive love they had for one another and the fullness it brought into her being. She sensed that it was somehow fulfilling to Him as well, and she was overwhelmed with emotion. She considered, *Who am I that I could share in this love, joy, peace, and freedom of life that He has known between the Three in One, long before He created my world; long before I was born?* And yet she knew she had been invited to join into this awesome relationship. Her heart overflowed with bliss. She felt patience with Chuck; kindness and sympathy toward Victoria. She was persuaded there was goodness, righteousness, and truth ahead. It gave her courage to forsake the shadow, the lie! She had been duped to believe that security came from property, family, and naïve assurance that she could fix anything on her own. But now, she knew. She could do nothing alone, but she was not alone.

A sudden cough jerked her awake. *My misplaced faith is in myself. I need to quit trusting in myself and start trusting you.* She said out loud, "But how?"

"Take up your cross daily and follow Me."

A cross, yes, die to myself. Okay, okay. Yes, I surrender and I'll need to surrender again tomorrow, and the next day, and the next.

Coincidentally, at her moment of surrender, it came into her mind what Johnny told her his mother said, "The Lord will provide."

CHAPTER TWENTY-FIVE

Who's Kate?

Every farmer knows, as at the theater, "the Show must go on," the Harvest must go on. They all would have loved to sleep in, take a few days to rest and digest the gold mine, sinkhole trauma and tragedy, but no. Tom, Sherre and Kate started early in the millroom. Sherre thought Tom's eyes looked clearer than she expected to see them. She was encouraged that he apparently hadn't chosen to drown the sinkhole experience in alcohol.

As predicted, the kids, including Tyler, who had a taped up, broken rib, bounced back, and went to school on Monday. Word was they were excited to replay the adventure that made the ten o'clock news on Saturday night. Deidre forsook the laundry pile and the dirty breakfast dishes and headed to her mom's to spend the day with Francesca.

Mid-morning, Sherre came out of the clean room, ready to help prep a small batch of Arbequinas that they were going to press for Jeff and Jennine Thompson. Tom adroitly maneuvered the forklift to angle the bin above the rim of the Pieralisi intake chute. Beyond the forklift, Sherre saw a caravan of vehicles climbing the road from the houses below. The gravel crackled beneath twenty tires. Leading the way was Denny, wearing his Stetson. His RAM was followed by a Shasta County Sheriff's cruiser. Behind the cruiser, Deidre was driving their mom in her mother's SUV. Johnny and Marcus brought up the rear.

All five people got out of their vehicles and gathered to the non-mill side of the millroom. Marcus respectfully sat in the shade outside on the gravel. Tom politely shut off the mill and the generator, and then joined them. When it got quiet, Kate came out of the refrigerated storage room, rubbing warmth to the outsides of her arms. She smiled and blushed when she saw Denny.

A look of surprise crossed the Sheriff's face.

Denny spoke first, "Sheriff West, here, stopped down at the Saloon when he couldn't find you off the highway."

Sherre giggled. "Yeah. We're hard to find. Most everything is addressed to our PO Box and there's not much down there on the road that says we're here." She pointed to the highway, and then put out her hand, "Hi Sheriff West. What brings you to Calaveras County?"

He took her hand and nodded, and then turned to extend his hand to Kate. As she accepted it, they said simultaneously, "What are you doing here?"

Kate giggled then added, "Good to see you again Detective West."

"Good to see you again too, Miss Lockhart. But why are you here? Did you hear, as I did, that your stepfather tried to kill another wife?"

There was a stunned silence as each of them sorted out Kate's last name. Sherre, of course, knew Kate's real name, but was trying to comprehend Darian as Kate's "stepfather," not just her own. Johnny's and Denny's reactions indicated that they both recognized her last name, connected it to her first name, and most likely, remembered her mother's tragic story. Tom and Deidre looked confused because the detective didn't call her Stryker, nor did they understand the reference to Darian. Francesca started to cry, and then stepped close to Kate to hug her.

Deidre moved alongside her husband. Sherre was pleased when she saw Tom take her sister's hand. They exchanged glances that lead Sherre to deduce that they had probably been physically intimate, but more importantly they'd regained their emotional bond. It was good. So good. She knew it wasn't about her, but a tiny bit of jealousy, sadness, and fear, that still had its grasp on her, released its grip so she could feel genuine joy that her sister's marriage would probably heal. Ahead of her was the hope that she would heal also. She would grieve the loss of her marriage and continue to school herself in all the phases of forgiveness ahead that would grant her heart amnesty to Chuck and herself. She willed the humiliation of rejection to fly away. All of that would come.

Time would heal. The only remaining trial was the fear of losing the Ranch, but she felt peace, knowing she was not alone as they all faced whatever outcome may lie ahead. The scene got a bit cloudy as she fought emotion, exaggerated by exhaustion. She knew the tears that wanted to fall were brought on by gratitude, joy, and relief that her sister and brother-in-law were emerging from the deceitfulness and lies that nearly tore their family apart. *Thank you Lord.*

Kate said, "Yeah I'm Kate Lockhart, not Kate Stryker." She looked at Denny, who was smiling broadly. Sherre realized that this was the first time that the great Denny Garter had a love interest whose financial worth dwarfed his.

Detective West said to Kate, "So *you* are the one that saved the new Mrs. Danville? The news said it was a Miss Stryker."

"On Saturday night, I gave the local sheriff my real name, but they were kind enough not to release it to the media. The rest of these people, except Sherre Granzella," she nodded her head toward Sherre, "have known me as Kate Stryker for the past month. The news crews interviewed others first and when they got around to me, it was easy because they asked if I was Kate." She smiled. "I'm sure when somebody takes the time to scrutinize the Calaveras Sheriff's report, there will be a media frenzy.

"So why were you here?"

"After you and I talked, I hired a private detective firm. I found out Darian was here, courting Francesca." She wrapped an arm around Sherre's mom and gave her a sideways hug. "I came under the guise of writing a book for the Olive Oil Council to keep an eye on the creep."

Francesca, wide-eyed, turned to face Kate, "So the reason you suspected that he was going to kill me," she wagged her finger between Kate and the Detective, "was because you both suspected that he killed your mother?"

Sherre knew her mother remembered the Lockhart story. She also recognized that Francesca was moving along beautifully out of denial and headed toward acceptance.

Detective West nodded. "I headed down here as soon as I could. This was my first day off. I never closed the case on Miss Lockhart's mother. When I saw this on the news, I was determined to uncover more about how it happened." He addressed the full audience surrounding him. "Would you mind taking the time to tell me more? I can see though, that I've come at a bad time." He noticed that Tom had moved to the olive mill and had begun to fidget with some dials before he picked up a towel and wiped the conveyer belt.

Denny said, "How about, when you are all through for the day, you come on down to the Saloon for dinner. My treat." He looked at Deidre, "Your kids too. I'll bring mine. Kathy's making fried chicken tonight. I'll alert her I'm having a party in the back room and ask her to make plenty of chicken and Portuguese Beans." He jerked his head, "Come on Detective West. Follow me again. It's a long time until dinner. I'll feed you lunch and I'd like to hear, if you don't mind, everything you can tell me about Miss Lockhart's mother and stepfather. This is fascinating." He winked at Kate, who blushed.

CHAPTER TWENTY-SIX

A Message from Grandpa Bob

The screen door of the old farmhouse wheezily opened and slammed shut. "Come see what I just did."

"Johnny, what did you do now? I don't know why you keep fixing up this old house that we may be forced to sell soon." The afternoon sun blasted through the screen door and splayed across the top of her grandfather's desk.

"Come on. Come see."

"Okay. What marvelous thing, oh Johnny! That *is* marvelous." She looked at the freshly painted new siding on the final side of the house. Next to the door was a little white box imprinted with the house number: 4044.

"Yes. It is. And look," he held his hands around the neat little box containing the house number. "It's got a light behind it."

"It looks great. Everything looks great. You know you've probably ruined the ambiance though, right? The sun, wind, and rain won't be able to find any cracks to penetrate."

He smiled, "And your house number will glow at night."

She bravely held back her rising emotion and said steadily, "Like I'm going to have a lot of visitors arriving after dark that need to find me. There's only a short time left."

"It's symbolic."

"Huh?"

"Your future's going to be bright, Sherre. Even during the night."

"How can you know that?"

"Because my mother told me and she's always right." He chuckled. "Hey, do you have a pencil? The lead on mine broke when I was leveling the house numbers plaque. I'm going to put in a doorbell too."

Sherre chuckled. "A doorbell? How about a security system? Do you think I need one?"

Marcus looked up from the corner of the tilting front porch where he'd been napping.

"Oh, I'm sorry Marcus. Did I insult you? Indeed, I don't need a security system when you're around." Then to Johnny, "I think there's a pencil in my grandpa's desk." He followed her back through the screen door. Once again, she pulled the drawer against a resisting scrape. "This darned drawer. There's something stuck in there."

"Lemme see."

Sherre slid her chair back to give Johnny full access to the desk. He closed the top of Sherre's laptop, bent down, put one long arm beneath the desk drawer and pushed it toward him, and then backed up to grasp it with both hands. He set the tiny drawer on top of the laptop. "Here's a pencil. And here's the culprit. He flipped open a matchbook in his hand. "It's got writing on it if you can call it that. More like scribbles."

"Probably my grandpa's lucky numbers."

"Nope. It says, 'look under the house.'"

"Really?" Sherre took the matchbook and examined it. "You're right. And it's in his

241

deplorable handwriting." She felt a rush of nostalgia at the familiar scrawl that she'd seen on so many birthday cards. Grandma Dorothy always carefully signed them first in her perfect cursive, and then added an ampersand. Then Grandpa would squiggle his signature beneath.

"Do you suppose there's something under the house that he wants you to find?"

"We've raided the cellar lots of times. There used to be a lot of dusty canning jars and some colored glass bottles. Deedee and I virtually wiped out that treasure over the years. I'm sure if there was anything worth finding we would have found it a long time ago."

"What about under the house?"

"You mean the crawl space?" She looked down at her feet as if she had x-ray vision.

Johnny looked at the retreating sun. "We've still got some daylight. I'll get my flashlight from the truck. Will you hold it for me?"

She felt the cold and smelled the rank stale air, then she heard a prolonged machinegun laugh. He reversed his crawl, backing up toward her where she waited at the little door beneath the front porch. He pivoted, and then continued his crawl forward, rather than backward. He handed her a rusty, two-pound coffee can with a filthy plastic top. Johnny's finger prints were evident where he'd opened it moments before. She backed up with the can in her hand until she could stand erect, alongside the porch. She switched off the flashlight and set it down. Marcus sniffed at the flashlight and then settled back on his haunches.

Johnny rose beside her, his hair and clothing entirely filthy. "Open it."

She did. She reached in and pulled out a silver dollar, and then looked up at Johnny's grinning face. "There must be over a hundred of these!"

"There must be at least a hundred of those coffee cans too." He was in full-on machinegun amusement.

Sherre started to giggle. "They're so old. Many of them have to have collectible value!"

"Um hmm."

She was giggling so hard she felt a tear at the corner of her eye and wiped it away with a filthy finger. "There was a song we used to sing in Girl Scouts, 'Make new friends, but keep the old, one is silver the other gold.' Now I have both."

"Well you sure have a lot of silver!"

"I have gold too." She looked him up and down, then said, "Wait here." She set the can down on the edge of the porch and darted up the steps through the wheezing screen door. She called through it, "I think I need to hire someone to repair this noisy door." She heard him chuckling.

"Seems you can afford it." He used one hand to vault up onto the porch and pounded some of the dust off his clothes. Marcus sneezed.

Sherre stepped through the door and stood close enough to smell his earthy scent. Beneath patches of dust, his face seemed to give off a reflected light. "Hold out your hand."

He did.

She placed the golden nugget into his palm. "This was a gift from a childhood friend." She saw a quick pulse at the corner of his eye.

"Seemed like the perfect gift to give the girl that you're in love with."

"Were you?"

He looked amazingly like Johnny Depp when he grinned.

CHAPTER TWENTY-SEVEN

Toad Haven

"Could I ask you to do me a favor?"

"I wish you would."

"I checked online. It's a burn day. Will you start a bonfire for me before we go up to Toad Haven?"

"Um, sure, but why before?"

"So the photos and other Chuck memorabilia I'm going to chuck into it, pun intended—"

Johnny chuckled his machinegun chuckle.

"—will be gone before we get back. It's symbolic." Tucked in Sherre's heart was something private. If it was not hope, it was close enough to be hope's sister. She made a satisfied gesture at the sky, as if God had prepared it for her personally after she asked for it. "This is a going to be a great day."

"Atta girl. Sherre wouldn't be Sherre if you had let disappointments win."

There was a softening around his mouth that was enough to make her legs go weak and wobbly. "Thanks Johnny. You may find I'm a different Sherre than the one you used to know though. Let's burn this fire, and then go up to Toad Haven to talk."

"If those tadpoles and tiny toads had been our children, we would be great-great-grandparents by now."

"Maybe we will be someday." Johnny lifted her onto their log. "Is that what you meant when you said you're different?" He looked at her with tenderness that she thought might be capable of erasing all the darkness of her past, then he sang in a beautiful tenor voice,

"You don't have to close your eyes.
There is room for love again."

"Johnny! I didn't know you could sing,"

"Marcus loves it when I sing, dontcha boy?"

Marcus lifted his head from resting on his paws and tilted it to one side.

Sherre giggled. "I'm not sure that look means he does, but *I* do." So many things were happening which made her happy. The stream went blurry as her eyes filled with tears. "Yes. That's one of the mantras that I've changed. I'm not afraid to love again and I'm not steadfastly saying that I'll never marry again."

"What changed you? Was it because you found the treasure?"

"I've found three."

RECIPES

Butternut Squash Soup

2 1/2 pounds Butternut squash
2 tablespoons Butter ← I often add more butter and a bit of olive oil.
2 sliced carrots
1 chopped onion ← I really like to use leeks and onion or sometimes just leeks
2 chopped celery stalks
1 large or 2 small garnet yams or jeweled sweet potatoes
5 -6 cups chicken broth
1 teaspoon curry powder ← I often leave this out
2 shakes nutmeg
Ginger ← I sometimes mince up some fresh ginger
Salt/pepper

1) Cut squash in 1/2 lengthwise. Seed. Put the squash and yams on a cookie sheet. Drizzle

olive oil on squash and yam/sweet potato. Bake squash face down in a baking pan. Cool. Peel. Bake at 350° F until fork tender, probably about 45 minutes to an hour

2) Let the squash and yams cool a bit, and then remove the skins.

3) Sauté carrots, onion, and celery until soft in 2 T butter. ← If I use fresh ginger, I add it here.

4) Add broth. Simmer for about 30 minutes. Add chunks of squash, yam, and spices.

5) Slightly cool and place in blender to puree. May need to add broth (or water) if it's too thick to blend.

When serving, I like to put a dollop of plain yogurt or sour cream on top and sprinkle with dried dill, but it's great just as it is.

Crispy Buttermilk Cornbread

1/4 cup butter - melted (half of a cube)
1 cup corn meal
1 cup flour
1/4 cup sugar
1 tablespoon baking powder
1 teaspoon salt
1/3 cup oil
1 egg
1 cup buttermilk

Combine dry ingredients in a bowl and mix well.

Combine oil, egg, and buttermilk together. Mix well.

Stir into dry ingredients until just blended.

Pour melted butter into an 8-inch square pan first and swirl around, and then pour in batter. If butter comes up on the sides smear it across the top of the batter.

Bake at 400° F until done - about 25 minutes. Can be doubled. (Then use 13 x 9 x2-inch pan.) Bake about the same amount of time.

Twelve Hour (or so) Pork Roast

1 whole shoulder of pork with skin (7 - 9 pounds) (Or, see the last paragraph of this recipe.)

Mixture for rub:

> 12 garlic cloves finely chopped
> Garlic salt and coarsely ground black pepper
> 8 small dried red chilies, crumbled (I have always used already crushed chilies, like the kind we put on pizza).
> Juice of 3 to 6 lemons, depending on the size
> A couple tablespoons of soy sauce
> 4 tablespoons olive oil (at least)

Preheat the oven to 450° F

Score the skin by slicing deeply through the skin and into the meat about 1/4 inch apart from one another. (I am not usually strong enough to do this but it all turns out OK.)

Place the garlic, garlic salt, pepper (to taste) and the chilies in a food processor and pulse until all the seasoning are coarsely ground. Or, chop by hand.

Place the pork in a roasting pan. Rub the mixture above all over the skin of the pork and into the cut areas. Cover all surfaces of the meat. Pour over the olive oil, lemon juice, and soy.

Roast for thirty minutes, or until the skin begins to crackle and brown.

Cover and turn the oven temperature down to 250° F and cook for 12 to 18 hours. The pork becomes almost shredded, crispy on the outside and moist from juices on the inside. It's ready when it is completely soft under the crisp skin. You can tell by pushing with your finger or poking with a fork; the meat will give and might even fall off the bone. Mine usually are cooked after 12 hours, but if you like it crispier, or perhaps if you have a huge piece of meat, you might want to cook it for closer to 18 hours.

Baste occasionally with pan drippings if you wish. If I'm cooking this overnight, I don't get up to baste.

I often get a much smaller roast that doesn't have the skin. I just cut back the amounts above, put it all in a Dutch oven with a lid and cook it at 300° F to 325° F for about three or four hours.

Ravioli

I don't think I can actually teach you how to make ravioli in the back of a novel, but if you are ambitious, you could probably watch a video to help you understand these meager recipe basics.

Dough

Bring a big pot of salted water with some olive oil in it to boil.

> 5 eggs - for each filling. Only 4 eggs if they are huge.
> About 1 1/2 teaspoons. salt
> Several cups of all-purpose flour

I use a Free-standing mixer: Crack the eggs into your bowl add salt. Start the dough hook at about 2. Keep adding flour until it starts to pick up the dough and wrap it around the hook. Keep "kneading" at about 2.5 or 3 until it looks smooth and elastic, scraping the sides and adding a bit of flour as needed. Mix together until smooth and elastic

Roll the dough into a ball. Depending on the size of your board, cut the ball into 3 or 4 pieces, form the pieces into balls and let them rest on another floured board. I use a 12 x 16 board, I cut the dough into 4 sections.

Roll the dough to fit the board. Smooth it with your hand as you go to make it shape correctly. Add a bit of flour as you go and flip it occasionally to make sure it's not sticking to the board.

On my board, I visualize four horizontal rows. Across the third row, place spoonfuls of filling across the dough about a half inch apart.

Get your fingers wet and draw wet lines between the filling and along the far edge. Pick up the edge closest to you and fold over the spoonfuls of filling to make little pillows. Press down with the sides of your hands between the pillows and along the top edge. Cut with a pastry wheel (preferred), but if you don't have one you can use a knife.

Gently lift them with a floured spatula and slide them into boiling water. When they float, they're done. Lift them gently out of the water with a large slotted spoon and set them into hot sauce to continue to cook while you make more.

Discard or set aside the remnants (they make great noodles) and make another row... etc.

Veal Filling

> 1 lb. ground veal
> 1/2 cup grated parmesan
> Salt and pepper
> 2 T butter
> 4 T onions
> 2 cloves garlic
> A small bag of fresh spinach chopped finely, or 10 oz. frozen spinach, defrosted and squeeze all the water out.
> 3 eggs (if I'm using extra-large, I often use just two)

Cook onion, salt, garlic, veal, and spinach until there is no more liquid. Add eggs and cheese.

Cheese Filling

1 small tub of whole milk ricotta
A couple of cups of shredded Mozzarella
About 3/4 cup of shredded parmesan
Salt
A little bit of sugar like about 1/2 tsp
2 eggs
2 tablespoons or so of chopped parsley
A few tablespoons of chopped fresh spinach

Meat Sauce

Olive oil
About a quarter pound of bacon
One pound of Italian Sausage
One pound of ground chuck
4 - 6 cloves of fresh garlic, chopped or pressed
(depending on the size of the cloves)
Garlic Salt
Black pepper
About a half bottle of red wine
4 large cans (28 oz.) crushed tomatoes in rich
puree
Basil - a grocery-store-sized bunch of fresh, or a
tablespoon or so of dried
Red cayenne pepper
A teaspoon of sugar

Cut bacon strips into about 1 1/2 by 1/2 inch
strips. Render the bacon in the olive oil. Take it
out and set it aside.

Brown the meats in the olive oil and bacon fat.
I usually do the sausage first, remove it, and

then brown the ground chuck, but if the bottom of your pan is larger, you could do it all at once. As you brown the ground chuck, season it with garlic salt and plenty of black pepper. When the meat is almost done, put in the garlic to caramelize it. Add the bacon back to the pan.

Deglaze the pan with red wine.

Add the crushed tomatoes, basil, more garlic salt and pepper to your taste. Sprinkle about a teaspoon or so cayenne in, also to your taste. You may want to add some water, or …

I rinse the cans with a bit of water, pouring them back and forth to extract the residual sauce from the sides of the cans, and then add it to the pot. It probably takes between 1 to 2 cups of water for my ritual. This is optional, but I lived with my grandmother for a while. She reared three children by herself during the Great Depression. I also scrape every bit of butter off butter wrappers. :)

The sugar is optional, but unless your tomatoes are exceptionally sweet, I find just a touch takes away any bitterness and marries the flavors beautifully.

Cook on low heat, scraping the sides, until it turns a brilliant, deep red. Probably between two and three hours.

ACKNOWLEDGEMENTS

Content Editing, Brainstorming, and Ideas:

Tina Fikejs
Sandy Isganitis
Tony Mangini

Map:

Alan Fikejs

Copy editors:

Kathy Anderson
Peter Bannan
Denise Davis
Tina Fikejs
Sandy Isganitis
Heather Randall

Advice and support:

Alan and Kris Mangini for invaluable Olive Oil Ranching research.

My cousin Denise (Granzella) McCarty and her family who said they'd be honored if I used their extraordinary Italian name.

Sherre Prada Bernardo, my high school BFF, for whom I named my protagonist.

Peter Bannan for help with characters, including his machinegun laugh.

Andrew and Tim Fikejs - video game screen names and wisdom.

Laurel Rourick for EMT logistical advice.

Formatting and cover:

Autumn Agrella Photography

eBook launch

P and G Graphics

The Map by AJ Fikejs

DISCUSSION QUESTIONS

1. Is it surprising to you that a man like Darian could capture the attention of someone like Francesca?

2. Why do you think Sherre didn't recognize that Johnny had always been in love with her? Do you think a long term romance can grow from a friendship or do you think it will never happen unless it starts with intense romantic chemistry?

3. Do you think, Chuck, Sherre's soon-to-be ex-husband, was sincere when he came to her home and said he wanted her back?

4. We tend to think of perseverance as a good quality. When Sherre was leaning toward making her marriage work "no matter what" because she wanted to keep her vows, do you respect her for that or do you think she'd be better off letting go?

5. What do you think of Denny's parenting skills? Do you see cause and effect of them in Tyler's behavior?

6. Do you think Deidre loved her husband? Can you relate to her in any way?

7. From the start, the Granzellas needed financial help. As you were reading, did you get ideas about where that help would come from?

CPSIA information can be obtained
at www.ICGtesting.com
Printed in the USA
LVOW10*0229180717

541714LV00001B/3/P

9 780962 762451